1-50

Recent titles in the *Torchwood* series from BBC Books:

9. ALMOST PERFECT
    James Goss

10. INTO THE SILENCE
    Sarah Pinborough

11. BAY OF THE DEAD
    Mark Morris

12. THE HOUSE THAT JACK BUILT
    Guy Adams

13. RISK ASSESSMENT
    James Goss

14. THE UNDERTAKER'S GIFT
    Trevor Baxendale

15. CONSEQUENCES
    James Moran, Joseph Lidster,
    Andrew Cartmel, Sarah Pinborough
    and David Llewellyn

TORCHWOOD
RISK
ASSESSMENT

James Goss

BBC
BOOKS

2 4 6 8 10 9 7 5 3 1

Published in 2009 by BBC Books, an imprint of Ebury Publishing
A Random House Group company

© James Goss, 2009
James Goss has asserted his right to be identified as the author of this Work
in accordance with the Copyright, Design and Patents Act 1988

Torchwood is a BBC Wales production for BBC One
Executive Producers: Russell T Davies and Julie Gardner

Original series created by Russell T Davies and broadcast on BBC Television
'Torchwood' and the Torchwood logo are trademarks of the
British Broadcasting Corporation and are used under licence

The Random House Group Limited Reg. No. 954009.
Addresses for companies within the Random House Group can be found at
www.randomhouse.co.uk

A CIP catalogue record for this book is available from the British Library

ISBN 978 1 846 07783 8

The Random House Group Limited supports The Forest Stewardship
Council (FSC), the leading international forest certification organisation.
All our titles that are printed on Greenpeace approved FSC certified paper
carry the FSC logo. Our paper procurement policy can be found at
www.rbooks.co.uk/environment

Commissioning Editor: Albert DePetrillo
Series Editor: Steve Tribe
Production Controller: Phil Spencer

Cover design by Lee Binding @ Tea Lady © BBC 2009
Typeset in Albertina and Century Gothic
Printed and bound in Germany by GGP Media GmbH

With apologies to Little Dorrit

I

THE EVENING
OF A LONG DAY

In which the events of last night are recounted, the seventh seal is broken, and our heroes encounter something quite remarkable

Jack, Gwen and Ianto stood in the Torchwood Hub, looking at the coffin. All around them, the vast space clicked and groaned as the storm raged outside. It had been a long night.

Jack reached out to touch the coffin, then drew back his hand and shook his head grimly. 'This is bad,' he said. 'Very, very bad.'

At that point, alarms went off. Red lights pulsed angrily, sirens whooped, and deep within Torchwood chimed the striking of a very old bell.

'But not that bad!' Jack protested, reacting in terror. 'No! No! No! No!'

It's a pity no one could remember who'd owned the buildings before they had been an air force base. But they had gone valiantly through two world wars, survived a few grim decades as a private airstrip, and finally they had become an industrial estate. But they had always contained a large amount of storage, which had long ago been unhappily converted into the Swindon Self-U-Store.

People kept a lot of things there – from furniture they'd never need through to books they'd never read. Old carpets came and went. Exercise bikes piled up like abandoned dreams. But, through all that time, no one had ever opened the door of Storage Unit Seven. Well, there'd never been a need.

And now, with the distant striking of an ancient alarm bell, the door opened with a gentle creak, and a figure stepped out into the harshly lit corridor. It was the figure of an immaculately dressed Victorian lady – properly attired from her well-polished boots through to her neatly tied hat. She looked around herself with grim approval and, hoisting her skirts up as far as decorum would allow, made her way gingerly along the dank corridor towards an area labelled *Reception*.

At the desk, nodding with late-night fatigue, a fat man in an orange fleece slept through a news channel. For a moment, the woman paused, watching the screen with a mixture of fascination and disapproval. And then she tapped the man smartly on the shoulder. Startled, he woke up, blinking, and looked at her.

'Good morning,' she said, crisply. 'I would like to know two things, if you please.'

He rubbed at his eyes and struggled to focus on her. 'Where've you come from?' he demanded. 'It's 3 a.m.!'

'I know that,' she said, smiling politely. 'But I would very much like to know the year.'

Without thinking, he told her it was 2009. She nodded with mild interest and tilted her head to one side.

'And might I trouble you for a copy of Bradshaw's railway timetable?' She started to look mildly bored.

He got as far as opening a drawer before realising that they didn't own such a thing as a railway timetable.

'It's of little consequence,' she sighed. 'There's unlikely to be a service until dawn. No matter. Thank heavens I have my *Little Dorrit*.' And then she expertly knocked him unconscious and strode out of the Self-U-Store and towards the railway station.

An hour later, she guiltily crept back in and stole his wallet.

It had all been a bit of an anticlimax, really, thought Gwen as she coasted over the last speed bump on the way to work. After the horror of the last few days, the alarms last night had seemed like some absurd warning of doom. She'd been expecting explosions, fireworks or the imminent launch of *Thunderbird Two*. But, after less than a minute, they had just stopped, the bells ringing out like a missed call.

Jack, hands clamped round his head, had straightened up sheepishly and realised Gwen and Ianto were staring at him.

'What,' Gwen asked, more sharply than she meant, 'was that?'

Jack laughed nervously. Which wasn't like him at all. 'Oh…' He windmilled his arms around. 'False alarm. Hey, it was nothing.' He looked as casual as a politician caught in Jeremy Paxman's headlights.

Ianto clearly wasn't convinced either. 'I take it that was some kind of warning system?'

'You think?' Gwen was oddly charmed by this.

Ianto nodded. 'But what's it for, Jack?'

Jack jammed his hands in his pockets and, for an instant, looked as though he was about to start whistling. 'Ummm. An obsolete failsafe. That's all. Redundant. Yeah. Defunct. Out of date. Past its sell-by date. We'll unhook it tomorrow. Hock it on eBay.'

He realised his friends were staring at him. Decidedly unconvinced. He looked down at his boots.

'Look,' he mumbled – actually mumbled – 'It's not like we need some flashy system to tell us we're in trouble. We know that. But we're handling it. And the bells and whistles – it's all extra stress we don't need.' He shrugged, and tried out a low-voltage Harkness grin. 'Don't worry – it's as outdated as Nana Mouskouri. If there was any danger, I'd let you know. Now – both of you – go home. Ianto – don't tidy up. Just leave it. Gwen – see that man of yours, find out if he's grown a beard. And get some rest. See you back here in the morning.'

He smiled. And the smile stuck like a greasy egg in an old frying pan.

Well, it was the next day now, and the world still hadn't ended. It was raining heavily, one of those grey Cardiff days when the sun's elsewhere. Gwen parked the car and stumped down into work, feeling the wind bite into her. She glanced nervously out to sea. She knew what was out there, and she knew how dangerous it was.

Rhys had sensed her mood and kept well back that morning. He'd been artificially bright, making tea and quiet conversation like they'd had an enormous row. She'd reached across and hugged him before she left for work. His face fell.

'Gwen,' he'd said. 'You look so sad.'

And she'd nearly cried. 'I know.'

She had to give him credit for being the sensitive husband while also guilt-tripping her into the middle of next week.

'You won't tell me what it's about, will you?' he'd said, eyes flicking away.

'No. No, I won't,' she'd replied. 'I'm too scared.'

She grabbed something hot and bacony from one of the shops in the Bay, smothering the white bread in ketchup. A little bit of cheap heaven on a wet morning in Cardiff. On an impulse, she nipped back into the shop and got two more bacon rolls. A little treat for the boys. The last few days had been so grim.

And with that, she walked into Torchwood.

Of course, had Gwen been looking in the other direction, she'd have seen something quite remarkable striding past Tesco. But no, she missed it completely.

***

11

With less than a quarter of an hour to go until something quite remarkable happened, the Hub looked as ordinary as a vast underground base could. A bit cold, a nip of damp in the air like a stately home, lights twinkling from workstations. Ianto was pottering around, making noise and coffee. Jack was prowling in his office. In the corner, Gwen could see the coffin. Jack had covered it with a big old velvet drape. It looked like Dracula's tomb. Not helping, she thought.

She handed out the bacon rolls. They took them wordlessly. Ianto carefully, neatly unwrapped his. Jack just started tearing into his, savagely.

I wonder when he's last eaten, she thought. *And I know he says he doesn't really sleep, but he looks like he could do with crawling under a duvet and staying there all weekend.*

Weekend? God, what day was it? Gwen thought about this, and didn't even have an answer. She was just so tired and miserable. The last week had been so stressful, living in a constant state of suspense, and too worried to even tell Rhys. She was shattered. They all were. How much longer would this go on for?

Jack and Ianto weren't speaking, she noticed. They were tiptoeing round each other. Almost like… no, they *had* had a row. And that was another sign of how mad things were. Jack and Ianto never rowed. Shagged like rabbits, occasionally shot at each other, but never actual couple-y things like a row. Blimey. She toyed with ringing up Martha. For a chat, a pre-wedding gossip, something boring and normal.

Jack strode away towards his office, wiping the bacon fat off onto a fistful of naval charts. He started making angry little pencil scribbles in the margins.

Gwen gave Ianto a sympathetic glance.

'He's frightened, isn't he?'

'Aren't you?' Ianto was talking with his mouth full. Another sign of the end of the world.

'I feel so helpless. All that work, and now we can't really do anything. Except wait for the worst to happen.'

Ianto nodded. And then he leant over, confidentially. 'We need a bit of a break, I think. There's nothing we can really do, is there? I was wondering about bunking off.'

'What?' Gwen laughed, and then shushed herself like she was in a library. 'Like nip up to the Red Dragon and watch a nice romantic comedy?'

'Or bowling,' considered Ianto. 'I mean, we could do that. But I was wondering about a Weevil hunt. There's a couple out in the sewers.'

Gwen grinned. 'After all this, yes. That would be so bloody normal.'

'Normal?' boomed Jack. He stood over them, smiling. Much like his old self. 'I never do normal.'

And that's when the invisible lift above them swung into action.

They all stared up, aghast. They were the only people in Cardiff who knew that if you stepped on a certain slab in a certain way, complicated machinery under the water tower would lower you down into the heart of Torchwood.

But the lift had opened. Rain was pouring in. They all ran forward. For an instant, Gwen had an absurd notion of a startled Japanese tourist, snapping excitedly away as they came down. But the reality was far, far stranger.

All of them stood there, open-mouthed, as the lift revealed its passenger.

Standing on the lift's stone slab was an elegant woman dressed in elaborate Victorian clothes. She was holding a parasol and a carpet bag, and she had fixed them all with a prim, complacent smile. She appeared unconcerned by the speed of the lift. She just looked completely at ease, like Mary Poppins' posher sister. In control. She seemed totally at home in the Hub.

Behind her, Gwen heard Jack use a word. It was, she thought, the very last word she'd ever imagine him using. It just didn't seem like him. But it was short, and rude and surprisingly blunt.

As the lift came to the bottom with a smooth click, the woman… no, the *lady* strode forward, reaching out a gloved hand to Jack.

'Harkness,' she said crisply. 'My compliments on still being here. Am I to take it that you are now in charge?'

Jack nodded. 'Like a bad penny, ma'am.' He sounded grim. But also… afraid?

The woman looked around her and fixed her eyes on Gwen and Ianto.

'Well, Captain,' she said, her voice purring with carefully controlled elocution, 'are you going to introduce me to your colleagues?'

14

Jack turned around, face squirming like he had a mouthful of slugs. 'This…' his voice dried, and he began again, 'Gwen Cooper. Ianto Jones, may I introduce you to Miss Agnes Havisham?'

Do you know what, thought Gwen to herself, bugger me backwards with a bent pole, now I've seen it all.

II

BLEEDING HEART
YARD

*In which something quite remarkable must account for herself,
there is sad mention of a submarine, and the domestic skills of
Mr Jones are brought into question*

They were all sitting in the Boardroom. Rather like a
loveless marriage, Agnes was at one end of the enormous
table and Jack at the other. Gwen sat tactfully in between,
and warmed up a carefully friendly expression.

Ianto brought in coffee. He offered Agnes a cup. She
looked up at him with her blue eyes and smiled brightly.
'Why, thank you so much, dear child, but could I possibly
have a cup of tea? If that is not too much trouble?' Her
smile widened a little more, and Ianto hurried away.

For a minute, there were just the three of them in the
room. Agnes looked around herself placidly. 'Well, this is
nice,' she said. 'Most pleasant, to be sure.'

Gwen nodded. She couldn't think of anything to say.

'Did you have a pleasant journey?' murmured Jack.

Agnes looked at him sharply and then beamed at
Gwen. 'Miss Cooper, my dear, did you know, in the old
days, when I awoke, I would be greeted with a carriage

17

or, in recent times, a limousine. Positively spoiled, really.'
She giggled. 'But Captain Harkness knows me better than
that. I am a martyr to self-sufficiency. I made my way here
using First Great Western.'

'Ohhhhhh,' groaned Jack despondently.

'Quite,' said Agnes. 'The seat had fleas.'

A silence settled on the room.

Ianto returned, carrying a cup on a trembling saucer
and a teapot. He set them down before Agnes and
scurried over to sit near Gwen.

Agnes looked around expectantly. 'Will the others be
joining us?'

Jack coughed. He'd once spent two thousand years
underground. To Gwen, he looked as though he was
contemplating burying himself again.

'This is it, Miss Havisham,' he said, eventually. 'My
Team!'

'Really?' said Agnes, and she looked at Ianto and
Gwen. Hard. And then back at Jack. 'Are you trying to tell
me, Captain Harkness, that the entire staff of Torchwood
Cardiff now consists of a woman in trousers and a tea
boy?'

'… yes,' whispered Jack.

Agnes reached into her carpet bag, took out a leather-
bound notebook, folded open a fresh page and made a
careful little note with a fountain pen, all the time staring
straight at Jack.

'There were two more,' said Jack sadly. 'But they died.'

'How unfortunate,' said Agnes flatly. 'I always

wondered what would become of this place if you were in charge of it. Not much, clearly. Next you'll be saying you've lost the submarine.'

Jack winced.

Agnes sighed witheringly.

'Sorry!' said Gwen, brightly.

Agnes glanced at her. 'Yes?'

Gwen tried out her best smile. 'Hello. Yes. Excuse me, but who are you?'

Agnes chuckled, a short, deprecating little laugh. 'You can't mean, my dear Miss Cooper, that Captain Harkness hasn't told you about me? Goodness me, what an oversight!' She clucked with amusement. 'Out of sight, out of mind, dear Harkness,' she said, and turned back to Gwen.

'I am Torchwood's Assessor, my dear,' she said, her voice rising to ring around the room with authority. 'I was charged by Queen Victoria to watch over the future of Torchwood. Whenever there is a crisis at any of the Torchwood stations, I awake; I take charge, I monitor and, if necessary, I intervene. My authority is absolute, my decision is final, and my judgement is impeccable.' She smiled. 'The machinery is most discriminating – it knows I am to be aroused only at a moment of great chaos.' She caught Jack smirking at *aroused* and stilled him with a glare. 'Now, don't be scared. I've only awoken four times in the last hundred years – and each time we were able to sort out the situation with the very minimum of fuss. I'm sure we should be able to muddle through admirably. Now, what seems to be the trouble?'

She folded her hands and glanced around expectantly. No one said a word.

'Captain Harkness?' said Agnes, her voice already sounding a little tired.

'Oh,' said Jack. 'Well, that was why we were so… taken aback at your visit. Not that it isn't always a pleasure… it's just…' He paused.

Oh my God, thought Gwen, he's actually frightened of her. She appraised Agnes. A few years older than her, tall, with strong, regular features and a stern expression. Normally the kind of ice queen Jack went for like a terrier for roast beef. But no… he seemed really worried. And sheepish. Wow.

Agnes seemed to notice her appraisal. She tilted her head slightly at Gwen and almost seemed to wink. Then she turned back to Jack. 'Yes, Captain Harkness?'

Jack scratched at the dirt under a nail. 'Well, there's so little on really. Just a couple of Weevils on the loose.'

'Really?' Agnes wrote something in her book. Gwen hoped it wasn't 'bollocks'. 'And the alarms went off purely because of that? How extraordinary.'

'The systems are very old,' put in Ianto. He looked about 12, thought Gwen.

'Why yes, they are, to be sure,' agreed Agnes. 'But I'm sure you keep them excellently maintained. All that brass and levers – must keep you on your knees quite a bit. I know how Captain Harkness admires a well-polished knob.'

Gwen spat out her coffee.

'Something to say, Miss Cooper?' asked Agnes.

Gwen shook her head. Jack was trying not to catch her eye, and she felt like she was back at school watching Willy Griffith getting sent to the naughty step for looking up girls' skirts. The more trouble he got in, the bigger his grin would get. Of course, once he'd got out of short trousers it had been less fun, but there was something of the perpetually grinning naughty 8-year-old about Jack.

Agnes shut her book. 'Well, well, well, what a mystery we have here! I've always loved mysteries. Still, while we're here, perhaps we should go and hunt some Weevils. Captain Harkness, I presume you have some guest quarters to put at my disposal?'

'Gwen will show you the way,' said Jack, dully.

Agnes stood, smoothing down her skirt. 'Very well, then. I shall retire to my chambers, freshen up, and then perhaps we could strike out for town?'

Gwen opened the door of the cell. 'Our very best guest suite!' she said brightly.

Agnes strode in after her, and sniffed disapprovingly. It reminded Gwen of whenever her mum came to visit. She and Rhys could spend about a week tidying the flat, and it didn't matter – her mum would zero in on a stray spot of dust or a tiny coffee stain. Only, in this case, Gwen could kind of see her point. The cell was bare, and clearly hadn't seen the business end of Ianto's duster for quite some time. A spartan bed and a chair were clumped in a

21

corner. The fluorescent light was buzzing like an angry wasp.

'Well,' said Agnes after an icy pause. 'It rather reminds me of the Crimea.'

Gwen walked over to the bed and started neatening up the sheets. 'I'm sure it's better than it looks,' she pressed on, making a brave attempt at a hospital corner.

Agnes took another step into the room, advancing towards the bed like a nervous cat. She sat down on the old woollen blanket, and, just for a second her poise quite deserted her. She let out a long breath, and her shoulders slumped. 'I am so tired. I know that seems a strange thing to say after being asleep for thirty years, but it's God's honest truth.'

Gwen looked at her. She just couldn't quite work this woman out. She just seemed so strange, so unusual and, just for a second, so vulnerable.

And then the cloud passed, and Agnes sat bolt upright. 'Well, Miss Cooper, thank you for doing your best.'

'Call me Gwen, please,' urged Gwen. 'And I'm a Mrs, actually.'

Agnes looked interested. 'So, is there a Mr Cooper, then?' she asked.

'Well, yes,' said Gwen, suddenly feeling she'd sailed into choppy waters. 'Well, no. You see, he's Mr Williams. I kept my maiden name when I got married.'

'I see,' said Agnes, and again there was a pause. 'How thrillingly modern that must be for you, my dear.' Her smile was a little too bright. 'And tell me – does Mr

Williams also work for the Torchwood Institute in some capacity?'

'Oh God, no!' exclaimed Gwen. 'He's a lovely normal bloke. He works in haulage.'

'Oh!' Agnes seemed genuinely startled. 'A drayman? What a rarity. One hears stories of these matches working out, but really you are quite to be applauded, my dear. Had I realised that, I needn't have risked that railway. I could have telegraphed on ahead and your splendid young gentleman could have conveyed me in one of his no doubt handsome carriages.' A tiny pause. 'Oh – that is, I hope I am not presuming… he does have carriages, doesn't he, dear? I cannot imagine you engaging in matrimony with a man responsible solely for carts.'

'He doesn't drive a horse and cart,' Gwen felt herself needing to explain, and also vaguely defensive on Rhys's behalf. 'It's quite a complicated occupation these days.'

Agnes nodded, politely, as though listening to the pretty song of a delicate bird. 'I'm sure it must be, dear Mrs Cooper.' And with that, she appeared to have settled the matter. 'There are so many things I really must learn about this future. All of them indubitably as novel as your domestic arrangements. Yes, how exciting it all is.' And again, that strangely childlike, mirthless smile. She smoothed out the front of her dress and reached into her handbag, Gwen apparently dismissed.

'Er,' said Gwen. 'I'm sure we can make it more cheerful in here. Really. Ianto's got a decorator's eye.'

'Oh, I'm quite sure of that, Mrs Cooper.' Agnes didn't

look up from her handbag. 'Please, rest assured – this room will suffice for the moment.' She placed a book down on a narrow shelf, fitting it neatly between some old bloodstains.

'At the very least, we can get you some magazines,' offered Gwen.

Agnes darted a crow-like glare at her. 'I have enough ammunition. And I am unlikely to discharge a firearm in here for my own amusement.'

Gwen shook her head. 'I meant... ah, periodicals. Topical publications. They're a great way of finding out about our culture.' I can't back that up, Gwen admitted to herself. She imagined Agnes confronted by the latest copy of *Heat* and shuddered. It had Kerry Katona on the cover, which was never a good sign, even at the best of times.

Agnes smiled her little smile and patted the book. 'No thank you, my dear. I have *Little Dorrit*, which will be quite sufficient. It's seen me through two invasions, one apocalypse and a Visitation by the Ambassadors of the Roaring Bang. I'm sure it'll get me through this latest jaunt.'

The explosion tore through the orchestra pit, scattering instruments and players in a tangle of wood, catgut and body parts. As the screams ripped through the stalls and the stampede began, Agnes Havisham strode through the smoke. She was looking for someone.

She found him, cowering behind a shattered drum. She reached down and plucked him up. 'Professor Hess,' she snapped at the shaking, coughing figure. 'This is your doing.'

The terrified man shook his bald head, his glasses sliding down his long nose.

'Please,' she said, her voice surprisingly gentle, 'don't try to deny it. They are here, and they are looking for you. It is simple mischance that you are still alive. I do not think that they will fail on a second attempt.'

A second explosion turned a balcony into matchwood and fluttering velvet.

The man shook his head, and stammered, 'Ich kanst nicht...'

'Oh for goodness' sake,' sighed Agnes. 'Kommen Sie mit! Wenn diese Kreaturen Sie nicht umbringen, dann wird es die Wehrmacht tun!'

Behind them, in the smoke, vast horned figures began to take shape...

'This is the maddest thing!' exclaimed Gwen, rushing up to the Hub. 'After the last few days, it's cheered me up no end, I can tell you. That woman is...'

Ianto gave her a brief smile, but Jack just looked blank.

'Aw, come on, Jack!' tried Gwen. 'She's clearly got no idea that her authority's gone. There is no Torchwood, other than you. And I'm sure her bark is worse than her bite.'

'Not quite,' sighed Jack. 'Agnes may seem like a crazy anachronism, but we have to take her seriously. Or at least humour her.'

'You've met her before, then,' said Ianto. There was the tiniest hint of teasing in his voice. 'Did it not go well?'

Jack puffed himself up slightly. 'No, it did not go well, Ianto Jones. And no, I am not going to tell you what happened.'

'Ooh, a mystery,' giggled Gwen. 'Don't worry, Ianto, I'll get it out of her.'

'We've got more important things,' said Jack. 'We have to convince Agnes that everything is going fine – it's a false alarm, and she's best off back in her deep freeze. We don't want her to realise what's really going on, or that the rest of Torchwood was destroyed or anything like that. Think of it as giving her a nice little day trip round Cardiff.'

'But why?' asked Gwen. 'She's a bit severe, but I'm sure if you sat her down and reasoned with—'

'Reasoned?' laughed Jack bitterly. 'You haven't seen that woman in action. She's like the Terminator in a bonnet. We need her out of the way. Quickly.'

'But all she can do is write her report,' put in Ianto. 'I mean, I'll read it,' he added. 'I like reports.'

Jack smiled at him fondly. 'She can shut us down with a word. Literally. It's called the Cowper Key. If she utters it, there'll be a total systems shutdown. The idea is that it seals all the evidence until Torchwood One can come and conduct a proper inquiry. But, with no Torchwood One…'

'What exactly happens?' asked Ianto, looking protectively at the Hub.

Jack shrugged. 'I don't know exactly. It's really bad. I mean, if we had Tosh, we'd probably be looking at days before we could bypass it and reactivate the computer core. If we had Tosh.'

'Rhys upgraded the RAM on his laptop last week,' put in Gwen. 'All by himself.'

'We'll bear that in mind,' said Ianto.

'Something else is worrying me,' said Jack. He was quietly tidying all the naval charts off his desk. Gwen also noticed the coffin had gone, leaving only the velvet drape behind. Jack had probably moved it down to the mortuary. 'Agnes has only woken up when the Torchwood systems think we're at a time of deadly peril.'

'Yeah,' said Gwen. 'She mentioned some of them – they sounded fairly impressive.'

'But,' he said, 'she didn't wake up when Torchwood One fell. A giant rift hoovering aliens from the skies of Canary Wharf? You'd think that would warrant a visit from our Agnes.'

'Perhaps the trains were bad,' suggested Ianto.

'Maybe,' said Jack. 'Or maybe that wasn't peril enough. I dunno.' He glanced down at the naval chart in his hand. 'I'm worried. I'm worried that we might be in over our heads.'

'So,' said Gwen, trying to lighten the mood, 'we humour her and get her out of the way?'

'Absolutely,' said Jack. 'Everything is by the book.'

'The 1901 Edition,' said Ianto.

III

MOVING IN SOCIETY

Containing the Children of Emo, an adventure in a horseless carriage, and Miss Havisham's brief career as an exotic dancer

Agnes strode back out into the Hub a few minutes later. She'd tied on a bonnet (where had she got that from? Gwen wondered), and was looking about her brightly.

'Goodness me,' she said. 'A Weevil hunt. How marvellous. I haven't done this for… well, depending on how you look at it, either a hundred years or a little over a month. How time flies when you're cryogenically frozen in a storage unit in Swindon.'

Jack, Ianto and Gwen exchanged guilty glances. They had been talking about her, plainly. No matter.

'Now then, weapons!' she exclaimed. 'Laser cannons always seem so unsporting. I think I'll settle for a decent revolver.' A pause. 'If you have one.'

'Erm,' said Jack. 'These days we tend to stun the Weevils and bring them in for observation.'

'Of course you do,' said Agnes. 'Well, I should still like a gun. Would you be so kind as to fetch me one, Captain?'

They stared at each other. Then Jack turned on his heel. 'Certainly, I'll fetch us all some weapons from the armoury,' he said stiffly.

'Splendid.' Agnes clapped her gloved hands together, and then spared Ianto a glance. 'And have your catamite bring round the carriage.'

'What?' hissed Ianto to Jack.

'Don't look it up,' pleaded Jack quietly.

The thing that kept the invisible lift invisible was what Jack called a perception filter. It popped you up in the middle of Cardiff Bay and made people look the other way. Oddly enough, it didn't extend to an immaculately dressed Victorian woman. Agnes strode through the crowds, nodding curt greetings to all.

In the distance, the Torchwood SUV sat parked. Ianto was stood by an open door, sheltering under his Snoopy umbrella. Agnes paused at the door and waited for Gwen and Jack to catch up with her. 'Harkness, you may drive,' she commanded, and then settled into the back seat. She patted the seat beside her. 'Join me, Mrs Cooper,' she commanded.

Ianto slipped into the front seat next to Jack and they drove off.

Agnes smiled, 'How thrilling the motor car is,' she said. 'Why, last time I remember being hurtled round Manchester at ungodly speeds in something called a Mini Cooper. Goodness, the 1970s were such fun. Pity about the dragons, but one can't have everything, can one?' She smiled at Gwen again. 'Of course, that was last week. Hardly seems a moment and, goodness me, they have neatened things up!' She wound down the window, sticking her head out like an excited dog. The rain belted into her face and poured down her ringlets, but she didn't seem to care. 'Last time I was here, the Docks were positively crammed with rough-hewn sailors, weren't they, Harkness?'

Jack ignored Agnes, driving carefully into town and steadily into the one-way system. Agnes looked around her with delight. 'My word!' she would occasionally gasp, darting Gwen a delighted grin that made her look ten years younger.

They pulled up outside a shopping centre. From sheer force of habit, Jack strode on ahead heroically, only to find Agnes standing in front of the doors, waiting for him. He smiled awkwardly, and held them open for her. 'Thank you, Captain,' she said and stepped neatly through.

Gwen, grinning broadly, ducked under his arm as well. Jack met her gaze and rolled his eyes.

Ianto waved the Weevil tracker around the shopping centre. 'They're supposed to be here, you know,' he sighed, shaking it until it bleeped reproachfully.

'Oh, there's no hurry, no hurry at all,' said Agnes's voice, faintly. She was standing outside a clothes shop, peering in through the window. 'So exciting,' she whispered. 'So revealing. Quite shocking!'

Gwen stood next to her, watching with quiet

amusement as she gawped at the shoppers inside. Agnes turned to her. 'Are these clothes really being worn by those strange children?' she asked.

'Uh-huh,' replied Gwen, watching as a tight fluorescent T-shirt was pulled over a teenager's chest, exposing a tattooed and pierced muffin-top.

'Are they some form of slave race?' asked Agnes. 'It just seems so…'

'What? Emo kids?' Gwen shook her head, smiling broadly. 'Nope, it's just the fashion. Honestly. Don't worry—in a couple of years' time they'll be dressing better, leading normal lives and working for the gas board.' *God knows,* she thought, *some of the things I wore when I was that age. I wonder if some of them still fit?*

'I see,' said Agnes. 'Clearly you must find me very out of step. And what must they think of what I'm wearing?' She giggled, briefly, before picking up her crinolines and striding forward, suddenly businesslike. 'Harkness!' she barked. 'Tell your protégé to put his little instrument away. I have scented our quarry.'

With that, she stepped quickly towards a door marked *Car Park.*

Agnes made her way swiftly and stealthily through the car park, heading across oily ramps down to the lower level. Pausing to sniff the air, she grimaced and indicated a rusted service door. 'Weevils are as rank as navvies,' she sighed. 'And they're not far from here.'

They stepped through, Jack carefully drawing his stun

gun. Agnes cocked an eyebrow at him. 'A careful aim is required, Harkness. I don't wish danger to fall upon the Children of Emo.' And she made her way cautiously along the corridor.

All Gwen could smell was rust and piss and damp. It really was horrible. There'd probably have been rats if it hadn't been for the Weevils. Lower forms of vermin just made themselves elsewhere whenever Weevils were around. Which was about the only positive thing she'd ever managed to discover about them.

Up ahead was shouting and roaring, and a smell of rotten meat. Lurching out of the darkness were two Weevils. Claws raked at the air as Jack threw himself to one side, firing off his stun gun. A bolt embedded itself uselessly, the cable snicked apart by a slashing forearm. Jack, forced against the brickwork, tried to aim again as the other Weevil closed in, but the snapped cable had tangled the stun gun's mechanism.

Somehow, against the roaring and name-calling and screaming, Gwen heard Agnes give an audible tut. And then she calmly aimed her service revolver and fired twice.

Both Weevils dropped to the ground, dead.

'Weevils bore me,' Agnes explained.

The horses thundered through the empty streets, the flickering blue gaslights on the side of the carriage casting fleeting shadows across shuttered warehouses. The carriage was very fast, the horses almost exhausted, but pushed on by a driver completely wrapped up in mufflers. On the side of the carriage, inlaid intricately in expensive walnut marquetry, and, lit dramatically by blue flames, was an elaborate 'T'.

Inside sat a man, who looked vaguely travelsick, and a woman, who seemed untroubled by their enormous speed. She sat, intently reading a book by the dancing blue light.

Suddenly, she stiffened as though something had changed in the air. 'Bother,' she breathed.

An instant later they crashed to a halt, the man falling across her lap. Eyes wide, he began to mumble an apology, but she wasn't even listening.

Something was flung into the side of the carriage with a whinnying thump. 'That'll be the horses,' she sighed. There was a scream from above them. 'And that accounts for the driver.'

She stood up, instantly dominating the cramped space, and silencing the man with a glance. 'Weevils, I'm afraid. We're going to have to fight our way out. Can you master a flare?'

'Why?' stammered the man.

For the briefest instant she rested her hands on her hips before regaining her posture. 'I am going to have to shoot them, and for that I need a distraction, which I am looking to you to provide, otherwise they'll simply tear off my head when I poke it through the canopy. And a flare will be capital – quite a noise, and the light will improve my aim. It may even summon assistance, although I rather fear we are alone. Now – will you be able to manage to ignite it by yourself?' She reached into a valise and handed him the flare.

Around them, the carriage was beginning to rock. The doors rattled and blows started to beat on the toughened glass.

She sat calmly down on the seat and began to load her gun. The man's shaking hands fumbled helplessly with matches. Very close outside there came the roar of a hunting beast. She darted an exasperated glare at the man. 'Here,' she said, and handed him her gas lighter. 'Even you can manage with that.' She took a quick look at her surroundings, and breathed deeply. 'Now, George Herbert – shall we mount our attack on the count of three? I trust that's sufficient warning for you.'

He nodded. She counted and threw open the ceiling flap, loosing off shots. At exactly the same time, the man applied the lighter to the flare.

It lit up the interior of the cab magnesium white, trailing smoke as it sped round like a screaming firework. Outside, the cries became louder, and one of the windows shattered, a sharp claw breaking through. The flare howled through the gap, driving itself wetly into what was outside. There came an agonised cry, followed by a loud explosion that lit up the sky and broke windows in the surrounding buildings.

She ducked back in to find the carriage filled with sulphurous vapour. Something wet and green was dripping down the walls and the miserable face of the man. Carefully, she slipped her gun back in her valise.

'Well,' she said, passing him a handkerchief. 'That appears to have dealt with them. You were supposed to throw the flare out through the roof – not let it off in here.' She smiled at him with surprising fondness. 'Oh, George Herbert, what are we going to do with you?'

Gwen only realised she'd fallen asleep in the bath when

she heard Rhys walk in. He gently placed a cup of tea on the side for her, then sat down on the toilet lid. He was grinning broadly.

'You're in a good mood,' he said.

Gwen blinked, picking foam from her cheek. 'How can you tell?'

He shrugged. 'You're home before midnight. You're in the bath. There isn't half a kebab on the bed.'

Gwen sipped at the tea. 'And that gives you the right to come in here? You realise that under all this foam I'm naked?'

Rhys nodded placidly, like she'd told him a not very interesting fact. 'So, what brings on the good mood? Or is it a Top Torchwood Secret?'

'Believe it or not,' said Gwen, and told him about Agnes.

Rhys stared at her. 'She sounds like my Auntie Joyce. You remember – the one we didn't invite to the wedding, and not just because Uncle Hywel smells of dog.'

Gwen ducked her head. 'Kind of. But more fun. Or maybe she's just fun because Jack's clearly terrified of her.'

'Jack?' Rhys laughed. 'So, your boss finally gets beaten by an Iron Lady you keep in the fridge?'

'Yeah,' said Gwen. 'And it's taken our minds off... you know... the other thing. The really scary other thing that I'm not allowed to tell you about.'

'Ah,' said Rhys. 'That still happening, is it?'

'Oh yeah,' murmured Gwen. 'The End of the World.'

And she giggled.

Her phone rang. With a weary sigh, Rhys fished it out of her jeans and passed it to her. It was Jack.

'How's your girlfriend?' asked Gwen.

'Agnes is fine,' said Jack brightly.

'She there with you?'

'Of course not!' beamed Jack. 'I'm as far away from her as possible.'

'Hmm,' said Gwen. 'Up on a roof, then?'

A pause. 'Might be,' admitted Jack. 'It's raining a bit, but the view is still quite something.'

'That's lovely for you,' enthused Gwen. 'So long as you're not looking through my bathroom window.'

'Wouldn't dream of it! Peeping's Ianto's hobby. I stick to Morris Dancing and shoplifting.'

'Any plans for what we're doing with Agnes?' asked Gwen.

'Trust me – it's all going fine,' said Jack, far too casually. 'She's an old-fashioned sort – she's thrown her weight around, had an outfit change, and shot some livestock. We'll have her back in the deep freeze before elevenses tomorrow.'

'And you don't think she suspects anything?' said Gwen, dropping her voice in a way that made Rhys roll his eyes. 'You know… about… The Other Thing?'

'Oh, she's suspicious,' Jack admitted. 'But Agnes is always suspicious. She's that kind of girl. And I'm that kind of boy. But I'm fairly sure she's got no idea about the coffins.'

'That's a relief,' said Gwen. 'If we can just keep it that way for a few more hours…'

'Yeah,' said Jack, 'We might just get away with it. Just tell me you won't say anything tomorrow. She can be very persuasive.'

'Not a word,' promised Gwen.

'That's my girl. Just leave Little Bo Peep to me,' said Jack. 'See you tomorrow.' He hung up.

Gwen handed the phone back to Rhys and sank back into the bath.

'Are you going to be much longer?' he asked. 'It's just I'm dying for a slash.'

'Oh,' said Gwen, and started to think about getting out of the bath. Maybe watch some TV before bed. Do whatever it was that normal people did.

And then her phone bleeped. It was a text message. Gwen read it.

'Dear Mrs Cooper. My compliments. I do hope you are well and would be delighted if you could please explain to me: what coffins? Yours sincerely, AH.'

'Little Bo Peep?'

Jack didn't even turn around. He carried on looking out across the city to the sea. 'Well,' he said after a while. 'That dress is very frilly, Agnes. How did you find me?'

'You've always found roofs irresistible.' Agnes strode out onto the roof and looked around, shivering in the wind. 'Along with, if memory serves, footmen. You can't resist shinning up either.'

Jack smirked.

'Plus I placed a tracker on you in the Weevil hunt this afternoon. Never waste a skirmish, that's what I say.' Agnes picked some dust off her shoulder. 'Although how you got up here is quite the mystery to me. It took me ages to charm the doorman. What exactly is a strip-o-gram, anyway?' She paused. 'I can only presume you have in place a complicated system of skeleton keys, bribery and sexual molestation.' She sniffed. 'Which at least demonstrates you're capable of the basics of organisation.'

She stood alongside Jack, following his gaze. They looked out, over the city. It was brisk, and the wind pulled at Agnes's tightly wound hair. She shuddered. 'This is a cold, high place overlooking the university. Do people really dwell in such towers?'

Jack didn't reply. They just stood, watching the night and listening to distant sirens.

'What is going on, Harkness? I've managed to unpick your shenanigans without even really having to try. It's best that you make a clean breast of it, and then I'll decide whether or not to call in the authorities. I'm not actually an unreasonable woman, you know.'

'You're not actually a woman,' Jack managed not to say. He nodded. 'Can't tell a lie, Agnes,' he began. 'I've been lying to you. For your own good. Really.'

'Really?' Agnes looked out to sea, and squinted. 'What is going on out there, Harkness?'

Jack turned slightly and shrugged. 'Let's start again.

Tomorrow morning. I'll tell you the truth.'

'From the very beginning?' asked Agnes.

'A new chapter,' vowed Jack.

IV

MOSTLY, PRUNES AND PRISM

In which our heroes start afresh, tea is taken, and disappearances are discussed

When they reconvened in the Hub the next morning, Agnes was obviously in charge. Jack had cleared out his office for her already, and now perched awkwardly at a workstation, looking like an adult at a school desk. Gwen couldn't meet his eye – somehow, she was convinced that the text message thing was her fault.

Agnes stood in the Boardroom, politely waiting for them to come in. Jack slumped in a chair, sullenly. Gwen sat away from him. Ianto came in, hesitantly bearing a pot of tea and four china cups. Jack fixed him with a glare that said '*Et tu Brute?*'

After the meeting, Jack took Agnes out for tea. Ianto and Gwen watched Jack, wearing a false air of bonhomie, hand Agnes up onto the invisible lift. And then the two ascended, like statues on a wedding cake.

'She is something else,' whispered Gwen.

'Something not entirely real,' said Ianto.

'I know what you mean,' said Gwen. They were washing up the cups together in Torchwood's tiny kitchen, an area Ianto called the Butler's Pantry. 'It's kind of like exactly the opposite of a hen night.'

Ianto looked at her blankly. 'No, it's not so much that. I'm serious – she's not entirely real. I've looked her up in the Torchwood Archives.'

Gwen whistled. 'That's brave, Ianto. She'll give you a slippering for that. And I doubt she'll go easy on you like Jack.'

Ianto flushed, briefly, and coughed. 'I just wondered – I expected her to be in the computer, but not, you know… accessible.'

'And?' Gwen was burning with curiosity.

'She's not. There is no one called Agnes Havisham in the Archives. She doesn't exist.'

The alien leaned over, its salted breath too close for comfort. 'It is the female of the species. Look at the weak thorax.' The voice hissed sulphurously, a tiny tongue darting across the dry, thin lips.

Its immaculately suited companion grinned. 'My dear Slyrr, it is just a woman. They pose no threat to man nor beast.'

The alien placed its stubby hands on its armoured hips and surveyed her curiously. 'Your women do not fight? Given their inferior construction, this does not surprise me.'

The man rested a hand on his cane. 'Fighting is not fit work for women. Every now and then one hears of distant savage tribes where women battle alongside their menfolk. But not here.'

'Indeed?' the alien hissed. 'And what employment do you find for them in your society? Are they breeding stock?'

The man laughed gently and looked at her. 'I am sorry, my dear. My companion Slyrr is somewhat lacking in the delicacies.' He turned back to his alien friend. 'There is an element of that, especially among the lower orders, but mostly they are occupied in genteel accomplishments, such as weaving and music.' His cane indicated her hands. 'See, such a lovely alabaster complexion.'

'Noted,' hissed the alien, its boredom clear. 'My question is whether or not we should terminate this specimen?'

The man shrugged, and looked at the woman regretfully. 'Well, in this case, I guess there's no harm in it. Sorry, my dear.'

The alien reached for the stubby weapon concealed in its belt. And then whipped round, alarmed. 'Henderson!' it barked. 'Where is my gun?'

'Here,' she said, simply, and shot them both.

Jack and Agnes were taking tea. Agnes slid her formica tray despondently along the counter, glaring balefully at its contents.

'You know, Harkness, this place once used to do the only proper tea in Cardiff. Crusts sliced neatly off of sandwiches, bone china, and table service from only mildly slatternly waitresses. How times have changed.' She glanced back at the counter, and then pointed at something sealed in plastic. 'Good afternoon. What is that, please?' she asked the smiling woman behind the counter.

'Why, it's a chocolate flake cluster, dear.'

'I see.' Agnes's hand jabbed at a boxed sandwich. 'And is that really a fresh egg sandwich?'

'That's right,' the woman replied, patiently. 'It's made in Merthyr.'

'That is hardly a recommendation,' muttered Agnes tartly.

Jack paid, and they found a table, away from the young mothers and old couples. Agnes stared in horrified fascination at her cup, yanking the teabag out by its string and letting it twist in the air unhappily before letting it sink back in. 'I can hardly bear to taste the tea of the future,' she sighed.

For an instant, that forlorn look returned, and then her face brightened.

'So, Harkness, I believe you should explain to me the truth?'

Jack sipped his tea and let his eyes wander tiredly to the forlorn selection of cakes. He was exhausted, and Agnes was the last straw. Perhaps, if he told her the truth, things might miraculously get better.

'Where do you want to start?' he asked wearily.

Agnes razored open her sandwich box with a sharp thumbnail, and groaned quietly as she lifted out the contents. 'Just tell me everything, Jack,' she murmured, lifting back the edge of the sandwich despondently and glaring at the egg mayonnaise. 'You can start by telling me why your outrageously lax operation hasn't already been closed down by Torchwood One. I suspect the answer will either be unpleasant or involve blackmail.

Again.' She hooked an eye at him, letting the sandwich flop back together wetly.

Jack spoke gently. 'Torchwood One is gone, Agnes. They gambled with the London Rift, and ended up with nothing but a smoking hole in the ground.'

Agnes flashed with anger. 'Stupid arrogant pride. Stupid, stupid, stupid. There is a difference between sensible exploitation and reckless, greedy folly. I always worried that there was a certain avarice eating at the heart of Torchwood. I'd see it, sometimes. When I awoke and had to deal with some crisis or other. And I'd see it whenever I looked at you, Jack. Oh, you're not a greedy man. But the people who hired you were. The kind of people who were hungry for results at any price and would do anything, use anyone to get them. I had hoped we'd learnt our lesson. Especially after what happened to Torchwood Four. It's a disgrace to our dear Queen – thank God he took her before she had to see this.' She brightened slightly. 'Ah well. To lose one Torchwood may be regarded as a misfortune. To lose two smacks of carelessness.'

Jack sensed an opportunity. 'That's exactly it, Agnes. Everything Victoria believed in had gradually been stripped away – and with overconfidence came carelessness. I re-established Torchwood Cardiff on the original lines – protecting the Empire from alien influence. We've done great work. Really.'

Agnes bit into her sandwich, her face falling as she did so. She chewed neatly and swallowed bitterly before replying. 'I see. I see. Well, I'll give your approach some merit for novelty. Claiming licence for your behaviour by the simple predecease of anyone who could have stopped you is certainly… well, it's an approach the Borgias would applaud, I'm sure. But not I.'

She pushed her plate away. 'The Torchwood I knew is gone. The Institute is abandoned. All that remains is this tiny regional outpost. I'm afraid it's my task to shoulder the responsibility either of realising your potential or of silencing the project for good. If you pass the Assessment, then you may continue your work. If not, then the sad end of this will be three strangers shouting in the darkness. A dinner of herbs indeed.'

Her hand tapped reluctantly on the plastic wood of the table. 'Is there anything of this world that has substance, Captain?' she asked, staring at him thoughtfully.

And so Jack took Agnes to see the coffins.

V

FELLOW
TRAVELLERS

In which the coffins are revealed and, amid the Yuletide
preparations, the Dowager Mrs Gowan is reminded that 'it
never does'

It was a ship of graveyards.

The coffins stretched out all around them, each one bobbing and clanking, tied together in long beads by swimming-pool rope. This far out in the Bristol Channel, it was an extraordinary sight – endless neat rows of shining metal boxes, somehow floating, rolling with the waves.

'Someone's been losing a war, Agnes,' said Jack. 'Somewhere far away from here. And they've been sending the coffins through the Rift. We've been picking up traces of energy-weapon discharge, but there's also some evidence from how tightly the coffins are sealed and marked that biological weapons have been used.'

Agnes turned away from the prow of the Torchwood speedboat and fixed Jack with her gaze. 'How many coffins?' she asked.

***

The Queen was very old by now and yet she just about walked by herself.

'They would like me to keep to a bath chair,' she said, her voice little more than a soft iron rustle. 'But I make do with a stick and a firm boot. These skirts conceal a multitude of sins.'

Her visitor leaned forward to catch the words, as courteously as possible.

They were in the gardens, facing out towards the Solent. Behind them, stood the house, grimly impressive in the December frost.

The old Queen took her visitor's hand in a tiny claw and stared at her with rheumy eyes that still shone. 'I come here every Christmas,' she said, laughing like dry leaves. 'A beach holiday fit for the Monarch!'

The threadbare grass drifted away into the lonely grey sand of the beach and the uncertain shuffle of the most powerful woman in the world came to an end. She stopped, looking out at the sea and said nothing.

Her visitor stood patiently, even a little fearfully, at her side.

'I am very old,' the Queen said eventually.

Another pause.

'Have I said that already? I am almost sure that I have. You will correct me if I begin to drift. Believe me, it is no discourtesy. My mind needs a firm hand on the tiller, otherwise it is prey to gusts.' The creases of the Queen's shrivelled face set themselves slowly into a frown. 'Yes. How was your journey?'

'I cannot complain, Your Majesty,' said her visitor.

'And your room?'

'Most satisfactory.'

The Queen laughed delightedly. 'And there I catch you lying to the Empress of India! Your room is so cold even the vermin huddle together for warmth. Am I not correct?'

Slightly abashed, her visitor nodded. She had found a small family of mice wrapped tightly under the counterpane last night.

'Well, no matter,' said the Queen. 'Your room lacks festive cheer, and I fear we shall not see the sun today. We are both women almost entirely lacking in the New Conversation. Even I find myself oppressed by the need for inconsequential chatter. Why, on the journey down, the Dowager Mrs Gowan pressed me for my opinion on the gramophone. I found myself completely at a loss for what to say, and so said nothing.' Another pause. 'When one is as old and fearsome as I am, a cold silence can be very cold indeed.'

A lonely gull swept its way across the beach and out to sea. The Monarch watched its passage.

'You are very brave,' she said suddenly. 'You know fully what it is that you have volunteered to undertake?'

Her guest nodded.

'I find it curious that I am in the position of bestowing immortality upon one of my subjects. I can feel only great sadness for you, my dear. You seem so young – and indeed, you will look very much the same for hundreds of years, I suspect. I fear I face my last Christmas, so the notion of being cut adrift from the banks of time holds a strange appeal. I have considered it, and, on the whole, I do not find it a warm prospect. You are certain?'

'I am.'

'Very well,' the old lady gave a little huff of regret. 'Time is a hill we can only roll down, my dear. You will travel further and faster than all of us... and... if you will permit the conceit, you will gather precious little moss. There!' She gave a delighted little smile, which her guest gave a wintry echo of. 'But you will be doing me and my Empire a great and invaluable service. The Torchwood Institute is a fine thing indeed. It has already protected us from wordless threats and given us technologies far in advance of sailing boats and gramophones. I know why it is that you are doing this. Of course I do. The pain of losing a loved one is something... well, it has marked my life. And I can see that you are letting it do the same to you. And I am old and cold and bold enough to say that it is the things we do for love that are the only proper things we do.'

They stood there a little longer watching the sea rush up the dead beach. And then they turned around and headed back to the house.

'There are about a hundred coffins,' Jack said expansively.

Agnes turned back from gazing out to sea. 'I make it eighty-seven,' she said, finally. 'And how long has this been going on for?'

'It's been a very long week,' said Jack, truthfully. 'We watch over the Rift – as soon as there's the tiniest peak in activity, we find the coffin and we chain it up here. We haven't let any of them go ashore. Apart from one. And no one knows they're here. Ianto's been doctoring satellite footage personally.'

Agnes nodded, showing the tiniest bit of approval.

'And have you any idea what's inside?' she asked.

Jack shook his head. A silence settled.

'Has any attempt been made to gain access?'

'Not with that sign on the coffin—' Jack pointed to a

mauve marking. 'That's a fairly universal indication of "Keep out! Contents poisonous!" Although, we've tried pretty much every standard analysis and a few other tools besides. About all we can get is a general impression that there's something inside and that it's no longer alive. And that's it. There aren't even any individual markings on the coffins.'

'No stony tears to mark my graven bed, eh?' Agnes looked thoughtful. 'They made the ultimate sacrifice.'

She turned back to the giant pens of coffins, watching them wash patiently up and down.

'It's magnificent,' she said, exhaling.

A chill spread across the boat. Agnes rested her hands on the rail and breathed deeply. '*Dulce et decorum est* – eh, Harkness? What a sweet and noble thing it is to lay down one's life for one's planet?'

Jack stiffened. It was almost like a trace of the old fight came back into him. 'It's a shame you flicked through two world wars. You missed quite something. A tonne of sweet nobility going on there.'

Agnes smiled. 'You shouldn't mock such sentiments – not when, as far as I can tell, you spend a fair bit of time dying for what you believe in.'

Jack shrugged. 'Oh, I'm lucky. I get to keep on dying until I get it right. Others only get one go.'

'Shame,' said Agnes.

They held the moment. It was as though Agnes was waiting for something to happen. She stood, staring again at the coffins, her face twisted in a smile.

51

'A remarkable, remarkable mystery. And you're quite sure that no coffin has made it ashore?'

Jack looked quite firm. 'Only the one. And we found it quite quickly. No one saw it.'

Agnes glared at him, full of sharp disappointment. 'I should like to see the analysis of that coffin. Not every threat is visible.'

Jack spread the naval charts out on the floor of the speedboat. He flicked on a portable Rift monitor, resting it on a corner of a chart. It hummed and growled like an angry dog. Finally he handed her a folder. 'There's the analysis,' he said.

Agnes took it, and leafed through it briefly, before handing it back to Jack. 'You neglected to mention something about this coffin, Captain.'

'I don't think so. Did we?' A trace of doubt crept into his voice. 'We were very thorough.'

'Of course you were,' Agnes's tone was pure honey. 'Within your obvious limits. Without a scientific or medical expert, how could you be expected to understand the trace elements report?'

'I really don't understand,' repeated Jack. 'There was nothing unusual on that coffin. Certainly no traces of life.'

Agnes nodded, sweetly. 'Well, of course not. But this report clearly shows an area of this coffin that's discoloured and where the metal has reacted, very slightly, with something. There are tiny indentations and mineral deposits. I'd argue that they're the excreta of some kind of organism – I believe it may have travelled pick-a-back on the coffin.'

Jack looked at her sharply. 'How can you tell?'

'If it was rust or mould it would still be on there. It isn't. It's walked off.'

'No way.' Jack shook his head. 'It could have fallen off in the Rift.'

'Oh, undoubtedly,' agreed Agnes. 'Or could it be that it left after it came ashore?'

'No,' said Jack. 'That's pure supposition.'

'It's a possibility, Jack. You've been collecting coffins. Coffins containing the victims of a war against something so terrible and deadly to life that they daren't even bury the dead on their own planet. Instead, they're firing them through the Rift. And you've been lucky. A coffin hasn't broken open and unleashed whatever deadly genetic contaminant it contains. So far. But that might happen at any moment. You've been so busy concentrating on rounding them up, that you've not even considered what dreadful creature it is they were fighting against. And that perhaps it saw in those coffins a way to Earth. It might also explain how that one coffin just so happened to drift ashore.'

'No,' sighed Jack. 'No no no no…'

Agnes just looked at him. 'We shall see, of course,' she said, and folded her hands complacently.

And, on the shore, the Vam awoke.

VI

A SHOAL
OF BARNACLES

Which is chiefly dedicated to the Glory of the Vam and the
regrettable transience of estate agency as a profession

'Interesting,' was its first thought.

It wasn't surprised to be still alive. The Vam had always existed – it would have been more surprised to be dead. Somehow it always continued. Even though at the moment… barely. A quick check told it that it occupied a mass of less than ten centimetres in diameter and barely a few millimetres thick. 'Interesting,' it repeated. What a comedown! Was this all that remained of the Vam? A creature that had wrapped itself around whole solar systems… reduced to little more than a splat on a… where was it?

It reached out into its memories, and realised that very little remained of them, and much of that was over-compressed. No matter. It would grow, it would repair and, when it occupied enough mass, it would unpack those glorious memories. It had no idea of where it was, or how it had got there. It tried out its senses, and

55

discovered it had very few. It extruded an elementary sense membrane and established which way was up. There was some form of landmass beneath it. There was an atmosphere – although it could not yet analyse that. However, an atmosphere allowed it to infer that there would be life somewhere. And if it could feed, then it would grow, and the Vam would live again. The Vam! The Vam! The glorious hunger of the Vam!

It stretched itself down, pressing into the ground… perhaps there was some food in there. Nope. Ah well. Something would come along eventually.

Opponents of the Vam would have laughed at its first prey. This was a creature that had eaten entire planets, which regarded the most impressive space fleets as a mere snack, and would casually drape itself around a sun. And the best it had managed so far was to eat a pigeon.

The bird had been wandering across the beach, and had noticed the shiny, shiny black surface of the Vam. It had been interested in its own reflection, and had wandered too close. Humiliating as it was for the Vam, it was enormously glad of the meal. Nearly every process had shut down. It was close to total exhaustion and denaturing. It was beginning to think the unthinkable – a universe without the Vam.

And then that pigeon leaned too close.

The Vam savoured its first meal in… no, still no idea. The meat was surprisingly rich, which boded well. The Vam briefly regretted not currently having a way to see its victim's struggles, or, more importantly, to hear the cries as it wrapped itself around it, and then the sudden, sickening *pop*! But it promised itself that soon it would gain some senses. In the meantime, it luxuriated in a first kill. Like a cat in the sun, it stretched out, and then carefully wrapped itself around the corpse, consuming every last piece.

It would, it decided, let itself grow a little, and also move around. Just slightly. A small portion of Vam examined the brain of the creature. There was so little to learn. Some impressions of flying. Water. Blue sky – which probably meant oxygen, always a good sign. Others of its kind. Things that were Bigger Than It And Moved. And that was about it. A pity, but not a complete write-off. The simple fact that the creature lived in some fear of persecution meant that there were probably predators. Good. It had been a while since the Vam had clambered all the way up a food chain, and it was rather looking forward to it. Slightly reluctantly, it unfolded itself from the carcass, laying it out on glorious display. Look at this, said the Vam, lovely bones for you to come and have a pick at.

And it waited for the carrion feeders.

By the time it made it off the beach, the Vam had learned a lot about this world. It had also grown pleasingly. Now the size of a deflated football, the sticky black mass rolled and crawled its way up the beach. Now it was mobile, it was easily able to locate tiny moving insects. Some of them were even blown onto it by the breeze. Breeze, it thought. It would be nice to eat something that couldn't fly. It had pretty much had its fill. It would like something more intelligent. Something from which it could learn. The Vam enjoyed learning almost as much as it enjoyed eating.

The Vam reached the top of an incline and extruded a basic visual sensor. Hmm, interesting. Much of what was around it was artificial in construction. Promising. Still, in the distance, beyond all the regularity, was a certain amount of natural life. Tasty. The Vam let itself look forward to eating all this new knowledge. Hey!

It recoiled, much to its surprise, as a moving box slid past it. Ahhh. A craft. It had been a while since the Vam had seen a craft, and then it had been something far more complex and deadly, a battle cruiser throwing itself at the Vam in a futile suicide run.

The Vam was transfixed both by the motion and the occupant of the vehicle. It would, it decided, very much like one of them. Another craft slid past, and the Vam wondered how to get inside one. It posited that they probably stopped somewhere to unseal their precious cargo. Ah well. The Vam rolled down the road in steady pursuit of the… Fiat Punto.

An hour later, the Vam had feasted on its first human victim. Engorged at such wonders, the Vam paused in its consumption, just long enough to learn the victim's name (Suzanne), all about the profession of estate agency, that it was squatting on what remained of her face in a car park, that she really wished that she owned a more reliable car, some worries about being late for work, an unresolved romantic attachment to a man called Brian and, while it was at it, all of her knowledge. Goodness, thought the Vam, what a meal, what a civilisation.

It drew itself up slightly and looked around. It was unobserved. Which was good, as it was still vulnerable. But still, it had to be said. 'Fear me, humanity, for I am the Vam!' it whispered, trying out a human language for the first time. It remains to be known whether the National Assembly would have been proud that the Vam's first words were in Welsh. But there we go.

And then the Vam looked at the remains of Suzanne. And decided the best thing to do would be to make sure that no trace remained. For the moment, it must remain unknown. It looked down at the beach and thought, 'Hello beach! Hello birds! Hello sky!' etc. And then it looked at the small cluster of 'buildings' and laughed. 'Hello Penarth.'

And then the Vam had a very clever idea.

VII

THE PROGRESS
OF AN EPIDEMIC

In which Captain Harkness makes a rash promise, and Miss
Havisham visits the luxurious dwellings of the urban poor

When Agnes and Jack got back from the graveyard, Ianto and Gwen were waiting for them in the harbour. Agnes was all silence. She stepped neatly out of the new Torchwood speedboat, the *Sea Queen II*, and strode away from the jetty without a word.

Ianto tied the boat up with an efficient knot. 'I think,' he said, 'she's very cross.'

'Yes,' said Gwen, helping Jack out of the boat.

'Hmmm,' sighed Jack. 'And she may even be right. I hate it when she's right. It's not just my pride at stake, although that's obviously enormously important.'

'Obviously,' said Ianto.

'No,' continued Jack. 'It's that when she's right, lots of people die.'

The artillery shell fell too close to the window, blowing glass against the hastily drawn curtains, slicing jagged tears in the cheery floral pattern. Plaster dust filled the room.

Jack pulled himself up off the ground, trying not to choke, and noticed Agnes already stood at the window, firing her gun at their attackers.

Jack turned to the survivors – all sixteen of them, huddled in a grimy corner of the room. They looked at him, desperately.

'Don't worry,' he said, 'We're going to get you out of here.'

And without looking round from the window, Agnes spoke. 'Captain Harkness,' she said coldly, 'should not promise what he cannot deliver.'

Finally, Ianto was alone. The Hub ticked away to itself, like an intricate clockwork masterpiece slowly, steadily unwinding. Ianto cleared away some stray mugs, and closed down a couple of abandoned computer terminals, straightening up leftover paperwork and tidying away pencils and pens into appropriate slots. Hmm, a slight smear on Gwen's monitor. Probably brown sauce. He'd give that a wipe down in a bit.

He breathed out, relaxing quietly at the thought of another day over. The world still here. Good.

'Mr Jones, a word if you please.' Agnes's voice rang through the Hub, and Ianto let out a little yelp of surprise.

He wheeled round to Jack's old office. The lights were off, but he could just see Agnes sat there in the darkness.

'Miss Havisham?' he said.

Her silhouette moved, an arm beckoning. The motion

triggered some lights into action, flickering across her face, which was smiling at him kindly.

'Mr Jones… Ianto… Come through, come through,' she said, patting a chair. She leaned over Jack's desk, plucking a boiled sweet out of a jar, carefully unwrapping it, sucking on it thoughtfully while she neatly and precisely folded away the wrapper.

Ianto sat down opposite her.

'You're working late,' he said. 'Well, you're sitting in the dark. Which is freaky.'

Agnes smiled pleasantly. 'Actually, I was listening to the wireless,' she said. She indicated an ancient valve radio, which was hissing quietly. She shrugged. 'Nothing on.'

Ianto leaned forward. 'I can retune it… Red Dragon is…'

She waved him away. 'It's on the correct channel. Please leave it be.'

And so they sat, awkwardly, listening to static.

'So,' said Agnes.

'Yes,' said Ianto.

'Have you worked here long?' asked Agnes.

Ianto immediately realised she knew the answer. She was the kind of woman who would have memorised his entire personnel file, even the awkward or curious bits that Jack had never bothered to write down. She was smiling at him with the pleasant complacency of someone who knew everything about him. Dangerous.

'I worked at Torchwood One,' he said.

63

She nodded. 'A fine place, which by all accounts came to a lamentable end.' The smile widened, and she adopted a carefully confidential air. 'I must admit that, at this precise moment, the Torchwood project looks like a noble failure. I feel that my role is almost redundant.'

'Why didn't you wake up when Torchwood One fell?' Ianto asked. The wrong question.

Agnes's face thinned. 'I can only suspect a catastrophic systems failure. I fear there's only a point in awakening the Assessor when there is still a Torchwood branch to save. Why, when Torchwood Four went missing, all there was was…'

Ianto leant forward, interested.

Agnes waved a hand, dismissively. '… an awful mess that we won't go into here. But I'm sorry for Torchwood One. I must admit, I find the entire situation a bit of a shock. Imagine. The last time I go to sleep it's the 1970s and, aside from some quite startling hairstyles, everything is in order. And then I wake up and find… well, it's like discovering the loss of the Empire. When I first went to sleep most of the map was painted a bold red, Victoria was Empress of India, and Torchwood were busily plundering the Raj. First time I wake up, I glance at a copy of *The Times*, and I think, *Oh dear*.' She leaned back. 'It's curious, flickering through history like slides on a magic lantern. I wonder if I've seen all I'm supposed to see, and feel almost cheated that I can't pop back and have a peep at some of the bits I've missed out on.'

'Well, there's always the internet,' said Ianto.

'Really?' said Agnes. 'And what is an internet?'

'Oh,' said Ianto. 'Well… um… a few years ago there was a project that linked up every single computer in the world to form one enormous dataspace of information.'

Agnes nodded. 'And it became sentient and tried to destroy the world?'

Ianto shook his head. 'Actually, mostly just shopping, dating and cats. But there's also an online encyclopaedia that's quite useful. And there's a lot of video clips. Again, mostly cats. But also some history.'

Agnes shrugged. 'Perhaps you'll be kind enough to show me this internet later. It sounds like a fascinating bagatelle. In the meantime, I was wondering if we could have a word.'

'Oh,' said Ianto, suddenly fearful again. 'Is it about the tea? I've been wondering if I should switch brands…'

'No no,' said Agnes, waving a hand. 'I can only imagine the trouble you must have with that bagged tea. No. I wished to have a word with you… about Jack. About… you and Jack.'

Ianto made a tiny, awkward noise.

Agnes leant forward, smiling. 'Am I correct in understanding that there is an intimacy between the two of you?'

Ianto nodded, looking as if he'd like to hide under a rock.

'No doubt one initiated by Harkness,' said Agnes soothingly. 'There is nothing to blame yourself for. You certainly wouldn't be the first member of Torchwood to be corrupted by the Captain's reprehensible morals. Sometimes I wonder if that man is incapable of forming a platonic friendship. He has all the swordsmanship of a Frenchie. It's common knowledge that the men of that country would seduce a table with an attractively turned leg. I rather fear the furniture of Torchwood is similarly prey to that man's depravities. But no matter. I do not concern myself with the despoiling of desking. As far as I'm concerned, he can slake his lusts on all manner of inanimate objects. No, rather it's perishable goods… it is you I am worried about.'

She laid a hand on Ianto's and met his shrinking eye.

'Do you have feelings for Captain Harkness, Mr Jones?'

'Yes,' said Ianto simply.

'You should be aware…' Agnes coughed. 'Well, it's just that I have known several of the Captain's companions. I've even met a fair few of them. My point is that those close to Harkness tend to die. He just isn't aware that his invulnerability doesn't extend to those he loves.'

'I know,' said Ianto quietly.

Agnes looked at him, hard. 'Well, I understand. It's entirely your choice. But I must warn you there's only one outcome. And I am sorry for you.'

'I see,' said Ianto, tightly. 'Thank you.'

And they sat quietly for a while, while the empty radio hissed away.

SkyPoint had once been the most desired address in

Cardiff. That had been before the building had started eating residents. And the recession. Now it was just another nearly vacant tower block in the Bay, glass shining from empty apartment after empty apartment. The Vam couldn't have hoped for somewhere more secluded. Suzanne's memories told it that SkyPoint was the least visited property on her books. (What was a book, it wondered. It would like to know at some point.) The Vam rolled gently along the beach towards the nearly abandoned peninsula where the once proud SkyPoint glistened in the morning rain.

At 10 a.m., there were two caretakers, one receptionist, and two dozen residents in SkyPoint. By 11a.m., there was nobody. It was 6 p.m. before any of them were missed.

A computer started to beep, gently. Jack kicked it idly with a toe, and then noticed Agnes watching him.

'Game's afoot, Harkness?' she enquired.

Jack stabbed the computer and it went silent. 'Not really. Just one of Toshiko's automatic alarms. Honestly, she set up so many of them, this thing pings at least once a day.'

'Indeed? And what's provoked it this time?' Agnes was interested in the machine.

'Well,' said Jack, scanning down the screen. 'It looks like a tag she placed on one of our previous cases has gone into action.'

'Unfinished business? How thrilling, Captain. Leaving things half-finished must guarantee you're always busy.'

Gwen and Ianto wandered over – both of them sensing a fight.

Jack, however, was more absorbed in the screen than in another confrontation with Agnes. 'Gwen, Ianto – you're not going to like this…' he said, beckoning them over with his grimmest smile that said, 'Well, you won't like it, but anyway…'

'SkyPoint?' Gwen had seen what was on Jack's screen. 'I thought that dump was pretty much abandoned.'

Jack shrugged. 'Even so, its few remaining residents, the caretakers and the unluckiest estate agent in Cardiff have just been reported missing.'

'Perhaps they all ran away together?' suggested Ianto, his smirk dying under the lantern of Agnes's face.

'A brief précis, if you please,' she snapped.

Gwen breathed in. 'Shiny apartment building. Tenants eaten by alien. It's been pretty empty since.'

Agnes nodded. 'I have heard many similar warnings about tenement living. It is only to be expected. But… how far is this away from where you collected that coffin?'

Ianto glanced at the map. 'About a mile. Oh.' His face fell.

Agnes nodded. 'So there may be a connection.'

Gwen shuddered, 'You won't get me back there in a hurry.'

'Actually,' Agnes turned to her and smiled. 'Can you drive an automobile, Mrs Cooper?'

'Yes,' said Gwen, alarmed.

'Good. Then you can convey me there. If you're too delicate to venture inside, I shall quite understand. Fear not. I have my police whistle and a Webley.' She strode off to the invisible lift.

'Don't you want me—' began Jack. The expression on his face was heartbreaking. And funny, decided Gwen. He looked like he'd been left off the school trip to Chessington World of Adventures.

Ianto threw Gwen the keys, and she caught them. 'Thanks,' she said. 'Don't worry – it's a false alarm. And I'll bring Agnes back in one piece.'

Jack grimaced. 'I'm not fussy,' he said.

In the setting sun, Agnes stood outside the lobby of SkyPoint. She looked up. And up, her eyes slowly taking in the sheer tall tallness of the building.

'So much glass and metal,' she breathed to Gwen. 'It's...' she breathed, '*ugly*.'

Gwen giggled. 'Ugly?'

'Yes,' said Agnes. 'I mean, I'm sure it's all very well for people of your time, but I must admit, I find this kind of building very... cheerless. Empty grandeur never really did for the Empire, you know. Shall we?'

The lobby of SkyPoint had changed remarkably since Gwen had last been there. Then it had been a shining marble palace. Now, it was a wreck. She couldn't quite put her finger on how it was a wreck, exactly. But the empty lobby, so cold, so cheerless, looked and felt wrong somehow. Partly the lack of glowing lights and ice-cool receptionist. But somehow… She shuddered.

Agnes looked around her, as though expecting the worst. She nodded grimly. 'Like the lobby at my bank.'

Something landed on her shoulder, and she gave a slight start, jumping back.

Gwen ran up to her. 'What was that?' she asked.

Agnes shrugged, craning round to look at her shoulder. 'I don't… I think merely a water droplet. No doubt the plumbing is deplorable.'

They both looked up. And stepped back hurriedly.

Where once there had been a chequerboard of ceiling panels, there was now an empty metal skeleton, tiny snotty strands of dissolved plastic trailing down.

'What?' gasped Gwen.

'I don't know, my dear,' said Agnes, coldly. Her gun was drawn. 'I am presuming this is not a usual phenomenon?'

Gwen shook her head. 'What is supposed to be there?'

'Polystyrene,' said Gwen. 'Polystyrene ceiling panels.'

Agnes looked blank.

'Er… a plastic… derived from oil… a…'

'Like celluloid, I see.' Agnes sniffed dismissively. 'I understand. An artificial material. And it's been consumed. Fear not. I am familiar with plastic.'

The wall behind her vanished, and she scrambled hurriedly for cover.

She turned rapidly to the worried-looking scientist.

'Let me see if I understand you correctly, Professor Jenkins,' she gasped, dragging him through the spinney, aware of the

disagreeably autumnal smell of burning privet in the air. 'This Torchwood training camp is almost entirely composed of—'

A plastic nun swung across their path and Agnes removed its head with a single shot.

'— entirely composed of plastic mannequins?'

'Er, yes,' gasped Jenkins. 'You're not supposed to shoot the nuns. Strictly speaking. And these experiments have the approval of Mr Chamberlain.'

Agnes sighed. 'Someone clearly bullied that out of him. So, these are here for the purposes of training operatives? And something has taken control of them?'

'Yes,' wailed Jenkins. 'They've killed everyone!'

They turned a corner and were confronted by a dead end in the maze. Behind them came an ominous stepping noise. They turned, and were confronted by the sight of a plastic milkman staggering towards them, blank eyes searching the air.

'Dead end!' cried Jenkins.

She tutted. 'One does not always play by the rules,' she said.

The plastic milkman fired at them, but they had ducked. The shot blew a hole in the wall of the maze. They ran for freedom.

Agnes glanced around. 'Anything else wrong?'

Gwen looked ahead of them. It was dark and she could just hear dripping. 'No lights… not even emergency ones.' She went over to the receptionist's desk. All that remained of a computer and monitor were a few electrical components embedded in a plastic toffee.

Agnes leaned over. 'How efficient,' she said. 'Have you a lantern?' Gwen passed her a torch, and Agnes clicked it on expertly. 'Fascinating,' she said. 'It's a long time since I studied protein strings and polymers, my dear. And I'm sure at the dawn of Torchwood we were scientific infants compared to you. It's simple, isn't it?'

Gwen shrugged, slightly embarrassed. 'Owen and Tosh did most of the science stuff. I nearly did Biology A level, but Mrs Stringer was a nightmare. So I did French instead.'

Agnes tilted her head. 'I see. This is a school qualification? Well, you really mustn't feel embarrassed. You've worked for Jack Harkness for over two years and are still alive. A commendable achievement in itself.' She smiled and gestured with her torch. 'We have evidence something devoured that computer most efficiently. All that remains could not be digested. Which tells us that metal is thankfully of no interest to it. This plastic… is it now of ubiquity?'

Gwen was still looking at the computer. 'Er… well, yeah. Kind of. I mean it's everywhere.'

'Oh dear,' said Agnes, looking smugly pleased. 'Then Harkness has got himself into a pickle. He's allowed a plastic-eater loose into the world. Let's hope it's not like an airborne bacterium. If it has a physical form, if it has to do work to find its prey, then humanity still has a chance.'

'What do you mean?' asked Gwen.

Agnes swung the torch around so that it was shining into Gwen's face. 'It has a varied diet, my dear. Along with some ceiling panels and a microcomputer, over a dozen people have been reported missing. If it is an airborne flesh-eater, then it is already too late for us. But we both appear intact. I suggest we look around this towering abomination and then head back to the Hub.' She swung away, taking the torch with her.

'Great,' thought Gwen. Immediately, her skin began to prickle, and she became convinced her flesh was dissolving. The sun had set and she was back in SkyPoint and she was about to be eaten alive. Again.

They made their way around the lobby, aware of the growing volume of dripping and creaking noises. Gwen pointed out a mostly digested electrical socket. 'It's been eating the wiring.'

'Ah,' Agnes nodded gravely. 'Domestic electricity. I've never really had a chance to examine the proliferation of electricity mains in the home environment. In my day it was still something of a novelty. Is there a socket in every room?'

'Several,' said Gwen seriously. 'It's throughout the building. Each wire is insulated with a plastic sheath – and it's been eaten away, blowing every fuse in the building. It explains why the lighting isn't working…'

'Ah, and accounts for that faintly sulphurous smell of conflagration. I suspect we'll find a small fire somewhere in the building.' Agnes looked alarmed for an instant.

'Yeah, well,' said Gwen. 'I still think we should have a quick look around, eh? Just a brief look on an upper level.'

They crossed to the elevator – not only was it not

73

working, but there weren't even any buttons left to call it. So they crossed to the fire stairs and made their way up.

'If only my parents could see me!' laughed Agnes as she led the way. 'I don't know if they'd be more horrified that someone of my upbringing fought monsters or used the back stairs. Ah well.'

The first floor was creepy in the extreme, like walking through a collapsing bouncy castle. The noises were building around them, and their feet stuck with every step. Agnes glared down. 'You use plastic in your carpeting?' she asked, quietly amazed. 'One would have thought that nothing could surpass wool, but clearly you have. I fear you may have become over-reliant on a single material.' And she tutted her displeasure.

Gwen raised an eyebrow. Truth to tell, she was getting a bit tired of this. Stuck in a dark, dissolving tower block, at imminent danger from flesh-eating bugs or of being patronised to death. 'Pity a smug-eating alien didn't land in the Victorian era,' she muttered.

Agnes barked a short laugh. 'You think me a little harsh? Well, perhaps. Every era gets the monsters it deserves. I merely observe that you have a superfluity of the material – which would make you tempting for something that preyed on it. Sadly, Wedgwood china never had the same appeal for an alien predator.' She spread out a mollifying grin. 'Bear in mind, a few weeks ago Queen Victoria was on the throne, Gilbert and Sullivan were still the toast of the town, and the biggest threat to civilisation was a revival of *The Importance of Being Earnest*. It's been quite a time, I can tell you. Really, Mrs Cooper, you must tell me when I'm being unduly cruel. Unless it's about Captain Harkness.'

'What is it about you two?' asked Gwen, intrigued.

For a moment it looked as though Agnes was about to tell her, and then she shook her head. 'He deserves that, at least,' she muttered to herself, and stepped down the corridor. 'Let's inspect one of these slum dwellings,' she muttered.

Gwen's phone beeped, and she pulled it out of her pocket. A text from Rhys.

Agnes glanced over. 'Your mobile device is made out of plastic?' she asked, intrigued. 'As is this torch... and neither has been consumed. Finally, something promising. I am beginning to hope that the threat has moved on.' She strode off, trying the door to one of the apartments. 'Should your device start to rot, or the light go in either of these torches, then at least we'll know that we are in serious trouble.' Agnes sounded pleased.

She picked the lock with surprising elegance, and stepped into the flat. 'Goodness, how deplorable the living quarters of the urban poor,' she sighed.

The last time Gwen had looked round an apartment at SkyPoint, it had been at its very best. Polished furnishings, mood lighting, the works. Now she found herself touring a flat by flashlight, with the knowledge that every step could be her last. It just seemed empty and rather sad – a sofa robbed of most of its leather coverings and all of its stuffing, kitchen cabinets sagging off the wall, bathroom eerily cold. And the wind. She shuddered.

'Someone has left a window open,' said Agnes.

Gwen wasn't so sure. She crossed over. 'No.' The floor-to-ceiling window glass had gone. 'It was sealed in with plastic.' They were only on the first floor, but, standing overlooking the SUV with no hint of a safety barrier... she felt a slight twinge.

Agnes nodded. 'All right, my dear. I think I get the point. Plastic is everywhere. I believe we've learned our lesson without needing to belabour the issue.'

They made their way down the stairs, the handrail sticky to the touch. Gwen realised her breathing was shallow. She was terrified, as though the building was about to collapse around them.

They got to the door, and Agnes paused, hitching up her skirts. 'Get ready to run,' she said.

Outside was the noise of rain – but a rain of glass, as panels, caught by the wind, fell down from the floors of SkyPoint. 'It might, just might,' gasped Agnes, 'be safer to wait until every window has fallen out. But by that time, I rather feel there might not be much building left.'

And so, with a shrug, they ran for the car. Gwen decided that, if you added the danger of being decapitated to the horror of being eaten alive, it really wasn't that good a day.

VIII

IN WHICH A GREAT PATRIOTIC CONFERENCE IS HOLDEN

A light supper is taken, in which a truth drug is administered, and the deficiencies of the Undead are much discussed

Agnes swept into Torchwood, wiping the odd splinter of glass from her dress. 'Jones,' she barked, 'I fear the carriage has sustained some damage. You will see to it, while I speak to your employer.' And then she marched past, bearing down on Jack like an avenging angel.

Gwen winced in anticipation, but Jack was all smiles. 'Agnes!' he beamed. 'What did you find?'

If his bonhomie withered under the strength of her glare, he did his best not to show it. 'I would like a word with you away from your staff.' She gestured to the door of the office. 'Take a turn with me around the room, Captain,' she commanded.

Ianto and Gwen stood outside, watching the row played out in mime. Ianto passed her a cup of tea. 'Funny day, isn't it?' he said.

Gwen nodded, and took a sip of the tea. It was horrible.

Jack's arms were flapping up and down like a bird and he was yelling, really yelling. Agnes's face was tight with cold fury, a gloved finger pointing at him sharply.

'Quite a woman,' said Gwen.

'Oh yes,' said Ianto.

'Do you think he's going to cry?' she asked.

'Dunno.'

They stood and watched for a bit. And then Ianto went to clean the car, and Gwen went to Wikipedia plastic.

Under cover of night, the Vam rolled away from SkyPoint. It had feasted. It had grown. If you had uncurled it, you would have been faced (very briefly) with something like a mobile football pitch. It had learned much from SkyPoint, sampling a range of materials and working out which of them it could usefully consume. Truthfully, the Vam could eat anything, especially if it was a threat (and then quite slowly), but it had a preference for a few materials. And it had quickly sorted out what they were. Food didn't have to be alive – if it simply required sustenance, as it now did, then this plastic was the perfect fodder. But if there was some life to be consumed as well, then that was joyous.

As the Vam undulated along the road towards Cardiff Bay, it considered its next move. What the Vam really needed now was a vast storehouse both of complicated polymers and livestock. Fortunately, it now knew about late-night shopping hours.

***

Gwen looked around the Hub. At Jack staring into a microscope, at Ianto doing something very pointedly at the other end of the building to do with paperwork, and at Agnes, staring seriously at a computer like a nun at a sewing machine. *In for a penny…* thought Gwen, getting up from her desk and crossing over to Agnes.

'Yes?' Agnes looked up, all teacherly, and suddenly Gwen remembered Mrs Wilson, who liked inviting the girls in her form round to tea. She'd choose four girls each week – invariably four who Just Didn't Get Along and force them to cram onto a Viyella sofa, sipping milky tea from Charles and Di china and nibbling at over-margarined malt loaf while Mr Wilson loosed off silent-but-deadlies in the corner. This was a very bad idea but…

'Fancy popping out for a bite to eat?' she asked.

Agnes considered it. 'A little light supper before things get really hectic? Why not! I hate thwarting on an empty stomach.' She stood up, smoothed down her dress, and looked over at Jack and Ianto. 'Capital idea. This is quite the best time to take an hour or two away for refreshment and reflection. We shall leave the menfolk to try and track down the threat. After all, I don't think Captain Harkness does his best work with me breathing over his shoulder, do you?' And Agnes winked, ever so slightly.

'Come on,' she said, 'I could eat a horse.'

On the wrong side of the River Thames was a supper club that was frequented only by hoodlums, thuggees and outcasts from common criminality. It was exceptionally hard to get a reservation.

The Waxen Maiden had squatted in the Embankment for nearly two hundred years. Its rooms were cramped, the air repugnant, and the food regrettable. The one consolation was that the exorbitant prices guaranteed the silence of the staff.

At the far reaches of the club, along one of the foulest-smelling corridors, under the noisiest of railways lines, was the most exclusive salon the Waxen Maiden had to offer. Mr Jilks had overseen this particular room for nearly three decades, turning a blind eye to frequent depravity and occasional murder.

Born, literally, on the banks of the river, he'd known only a life of fighting and villainy. His face was latticed with scars, and his lips were twisted into a drooling grin. It was rare that he was beaten in a fight.

Tonight he was on extra vigilance. His guests were important, and he was standing guard outside with young Conradin, a man with the olive complexion and all the vices of the Turk.

Inside the salon, Mrs Magee was hurriedly ladling out a broth into worn china bowls before beating a hasty retreat. A collection of figures in suits sat staring at the remarkable man who was addressing them.

He was remarkably tall and portly, rather like a beer barrel wrapped in velvet. He had long white hair and an orange beard, and smoked glasses that flashed dangerously in the candlelight.

A portrait of the late Queen hung over the soot-encrusted fireplace, draped with a black sash.

'In celebration of the accession of our beloved King, I have thrown together this supper club. This is a time when nations change like seasons, and empires quiver and fall like leaves in autumn. It is a period that can be marked only by a meal of great moment. You are aware that the dish of which you are about to partake is unique. No one has ever, in the history of time, eaten such a thing. You are all epicureans who have paid handsomely for this privilege, and you are to be richly rewarded. Even I have not tasted this creature yet.'

He gestured to something in the corner that rustled and twitched.

'If only Mr Darwin could have been at our table. I've read in his journals that he feasted on Dodo. How he'd have enjoyed eating this... a creature from beyond our world.'

And he looked around the table and smiled. There was dutiful applause. The man bowed.

He picked up a sharp knife and pointed to the assembled diners. 'I think the honour of preparing this alien should go to...' The knife waved across the room and settled on a figure. 'Well, Madam Squeers, as the only lady present... would you care to make the first cut?'

The woman stood, bowing stiffly, and acknowledging the jealous murmurs of the others at the table.

She took the knife ceremonially and observed it coolly. And then she turned to the diners.

'It will be an honour,' she said.

And she looked up, her face caught in the flickering light.

The tall man gasped. 'You... you're not...'

The knife made only the tiniest noise as it whispered past his windpipe, before making several darting movements around the table.

It was all over in seconds. The woman surveyed the diners

81

slumped over the table, and cocked an ear to check that she hadn't alerted either Jilks or Conradin.

She dipped a finger in the soup and tasted it. Too salty.

She turned, and advanced on the figure in the corner. It rattled with alarm, but she held the knife up to her mouth in a shushing gesture. 'I am here to help,' she said, bending down and slicing through the cords that bound it.

As she stood back, the alien unfolded, twitching arms like branches spreading out from a body made of toadstools and mossy tree bark. It shuffled towards her, sharp leaves whipping through the air. For a second, it looked like it was about to fall on the woman, and then it paused. Waiting.

She looked at it calmly, and spoke. 'My names is Agnes Havisham,' she said. 'We have received your message. Help is on the way.'

They strode out of Torchwood into a night down the Bay. It was early evening – post-work drinkers trying not to stare at the woman in crinolines before deciding she was probably promoting a tourist attraction.

Gwen found them a cocktail bar/club/dim-sum parlour where the service was unobtrusive to the point of being non-existent. Agnes stared happily out across the Bay.

Gwen ordered beer for herself and tea for Agnes, then sat back. Mustn't make it look like an interrogation, she told herself. And yawned happily. 'What do you think of Cardiff?' she asked.

'Oh, magnificent what's been managed here, don't you

think, my dear?' Agnes said. 'Cardiff really has made itself. Why, I remember the first time I came here was in… ooh, turn of the century before last. That Rift had opened up and the dead were walking the streets. Apparently it wasn't the first time. Well, that was the local legend, anyway. Honestly, you'd have loved it – taking pot shots at the Undead without their grieving loved ones noticing. Oh, the mess!' Agnes laughed, as though it brought back fond memories.

'Oh, Zombies!' Gwen laughed as well. 'God, they're the worst, aren't they?'

'Ah, you've met the Undead? No conversation!' Agnes smiled.

'Yeah, and no real plan other than shuffling around, eating people and stinking the place out.'

'Tiresome,' Agnes agreed. 'And requires no end of explaining away.'

'Oh, we don't really bother with that so much these days,' said Gwen.

'What, my dear?' Agnes's cup paused halfway to her lips, and her eyes narrowed dangerously.

'Well, these days the whole alien cat is rather out of the bag.'

'Am I to reprimand Captain Harkness for this?' Agnes asked.

'Oh no. The Daleks invaded.'

'Goodness!' Agnes gasped. 'I've seen lithographs, but never come across such fearsome mechanicals! And have you?'

'Horrible,' said Gwen. 'But after that... well, everyone kind of knows about aliens. We still try and keep Torchwood a bit secret. But, you know, alien invasions and so on are now a bit like a rubbish one-night stand, you know. Everyone just prefers not to talk about it.'

'I see,' said Agnes. 'And what is a one-night stand?'

'Ah,' said Gwen.

Agnes poured herself a cup of Chinese tea and noticed, with interest, the bottle of beer Gwen was necking. Her calculating look suggested that drinking straight from the bottle was somehow a little wrong.

Gwen made another guess. 'And Torchwood Cardiff – what was it like in the early days?'

'Well, my dear...' Agnes looked thrilled to be asked. 'Actually, I was influential in getting Cardiff a Torchwood base, don't you know? It was before I became the Assessor – when I was down here shooting at zombies. I thought, "This thing's 'appened before, and it may well 'appen again, Aggie, you mark my words."' She coughed slightly, and her voice resumed its normal timbre. 'And I realised the Rift was strong enough and still very much dangerous. It was as though it had lain dormant for millennia but some space-time disturbance a few years earlier had just... shifted it slightly. Awoken it, you might say. Curious.'

'I see,' said Gwen.

'And I was right – from then on it was... oh, you know. Elizabethan plague doctors walking the streets, a litter of alien objects, strange lights in the sky...'

'Business as usual,' smiled Gwen.

'Quite,' said Agnes, echoing the smile. She looked around the bar. 'Oh yes, it couldn't happen to a nicer city. And there was this gal up in Scotland, Alice Guppy. Dear creature, very bright, serious as the tomb, but couldn't hold a teacup without crooking her little finger. No one knew what to do with her... And so we shipped her down here.' She turned in her seat and glared at a passing waitress, who slouched over. 'My dear,' smiled Agnes, 'I don't suppose you have a sherry, do you?'

'End of the bloody world,' sighed Jack, prodding at the decomposing sample.

Ianto looked up from neatening Gwen's desk. 'Jack?'

'That woman.' Jack's tone was sour. He rearranged his braces, distractedly, which gave him the air of an old-fashioned comedian about to tell a joke about his mother-in-law. 'Why does she always have to be right?'

Ianto gently laid a hand on Jack's shoulder. 'Because otherwise she wouldn't be so annoying.'

And Jack took the hand, and smiled.

'And what, pray, is this?' giggled Agnes. She'd untied her bonnet and it rested unsteadily on the seat next to them. She stared curiously at the tiny glass in front of her. 'It seems but a thimble, yet it savours rather strongly of spirits.' She looked at Gwen with mock disapproval, and then hiccupped. 'Oh dear, I'm afraid I'm getting a bit Mrs Gaskell in my cups.' She raised the glass, sniffed at it again, and then downed it in one with barely a shudder. 'Nope. My father taught me, quietly, all the various types of rum and it most certainly isn't of those. He feared I would take after mama's Scottish heritage and was keen to teach me about things other than a single malt. Which,' her face flushed, 'isn't really what a father is supposed to distil in his offspring – instil rather – only… oh, he so wanted a son and was delighted when I could shoot straight.'

Gwen sipped carefully at her zambuca. The Welsh truth serum was working its wonders.

'Why another!' roared Agnes, happily, slapping the table and startling a waitress into action. 'There's a liquorice savour about it which rather tickles the… Why, Mrs Cooper, I declare you have me tipsy.' And a slow smile spread across her features. 'I know what you're doing, you know,' she said, slyly.

'What?' Gwen decided on mock innocence. 'Don't know what you're talking about.'

'You are trying to get me inebriated in hopes that I'll tell you about myself. There's no need to worry – I'll gladly tell you whatever you want to know. Consider me an open book, my dear friend.'

And Agnes plucked refilled glasses from a tray and used a gloved hand to wave away the waitress.

'So you don't mind me dragging you out and getting you drunk?'

'Not at all!' Agnes laughed. Around them the Bay was filling up, as the residents realised it wasn't going to rain after all, and so decided to make the most of a reasonable evening, wandering from bar to restaurant to bar, sitting wrapped up outside to smoke in the icy air, or crammed up against a variety of over-designed tables.

Agnes looked around and sighed. 'Oh dear, I sound most approving of all of this debauch. I must tell you, I think there is nothing sadder than the belief that a good time can be had solely with alcoholic beverages and associating with people of only the very lowest sort.'

'Quite right,' said Gwen and they clinked glasses.

They smiled at each other across the table.

'Pump away, dear friend,' said Agnes.

'Well, you were a proper Torchwood agent?'

Agnes nodded solemnly. 'Absolutely.'

'Well... how did your parents feel about you joining Torchwood. I mean, surely...'

'Oh...' Agnes looked melancholy for a second. 'Best not, dear Mrs Cooper. Ask me another.'

'It's just... Well, you're not in the computer.'

Agnes wagged a mildly drunken finger. 'Naughty Mrs Cooper. But of course I'm not. Well, I am, but you see... Agnes Havisham isn't my real name.'

'Oh,' said Gwen.

'Ah. Late 1901 it was, when the chamber was finally prepared. When I became the Assessor, it was decided to leave all that behind. After all, if I have a past, how can I control the future?'

'That's a bit... pompous?'

'Ah.' Agnes tapped the side of her nose. 'It was a pronouncement of Victoria Regina herself.'

'You knew her?' Gwen gasped.

'Oh, just a little, and she was as mad as a box of March hares by then… but yes. Frighteningly intimidating woman. And, wherever she went, the rustle rustle rustle of all those skirts. And the smell of naphtha. Actually, underneath all the starch and cobwebs, she had a wicked sense of humour. She let me pick my own name… and it was either Agnes Havisham or Betsey Trotwood.'

'But your real name…?'

'Ohhh,' Agnes sighed, and pushed a hand through her hair. 'It's so long ago and I don't think it matters to anyone. It was just one more thing to give up in the line of duty.'

'Well,' said Gwen. 'You are remarkable.'

'Why thank you, but that's not a question.'

'That's not quite what I meant. You see… you come from a time when independent women were few and far between… you know.'

'Oh, dashed Florence and her blessed lamp!'

'Exactly. And yet… you…'

'Fought monsters and foiled conspiracies and blew really big things to smithereens. The real thing, you might say!'

'Yes. But what made you give it up? I mean, to assign yourself to… well, leaving your entire life behind, to living out history?'

'Ohhhhhhh, the big one.' Agnes stared at the glass in front of her and sighed. 'Every time I sleep, it seems I wake up in another time… and I feel more and more out of my depth. Especially now that Jack tells me that I'm alone. That you three are all that remains of Torchwood. It really...' She drained the glass, banged it on the table, and suddenly stared sharply at Gwen. 'I did it for love, you know.'

'Really?' Gwen smiled. 'It's just that Love and Torchwood aren't exactly...'

'Well, exactly. Oh, don't worry, my dear, he didn't die... no, it was worse.' Agnes settled back in her chair, and begin to fiddle with the placemats. 'You see, he was... George Herbert Sanderson. He was a brilliant young scientist at Torchwood. A brain to be protected. And we were very much in love. However, he was working on a stardrive that had been recovered from a ship. And, believe it or not, he repaired it. He even managed to work out the planet of origin. A distant world of riches and wonders who were in need of assistance. And he asked permission to voyage there on behalf of the British Empire. Victoria herself, the dear Queen, was delighted by the novelty of the concept, although it would come to fruition only long after she passed through the veil. You see, my dear, George's journey, even with this drive, would take him a long time. Over a hundred years. I asked him not to go, but he looked at me, and I knew that there would be no dissuading him. And sometimes you have to let them go... But I never give up without a fight. So, when the post of Assessor came up, I volunteered for it. I waved off his rocket ship, knowing full well that one day I would be there when he returned, God willing. And really, it works out rather well… in its own peculiar way. He's awake but the speeds he travels at rather bend time. It's all rather complex. Suffice it to say that whenever I am awake I can communicate with him via radioscope. I can hear his voice and he can hear mine. And there we are, two lovers split by time and space. But one day, he will return. And I'll make sure that this world is in good shape for him.'

Gwen just stared at Agnes.

'Have I said too much?' asked Agnes.

'No,' said Gwen. 'Wow.'

'But it is a most elegant solution, is it not?'

'You've certainly got balls, that's all I'll say.'

Agnes smiled. 'I think you've had quite enough to drink, my dear.'

'No, really,' said Gwen, reaching out an arm and hoping to catch a waitress. 'One more before we go back. I think we can grab a pizza on the way. You see, there's one more thing I'm dying to ask you.' And she giggled and leaned forward. Agnes did too. 'You and… Well, it's about Jack. Tell me about him.'

'Ah,' said Agnes, and her smile stretched. 'Captain Jack Harkness. Well, I can tell you that he's hammering on the window.'

IX

WHO PASSES BY
THIS ROAD SO LATE?

In which Miss Rogers fails to purchase a train set,
and a siege is laid

She'd always liked toy shops. Nina Rogers skipped a few
tracks on her MP3 player and looked around her. Every
aisle was a different dream – teddy bears, board games,
princess outfits, racer bikes, football kits and train sets.
She was watching an elaborately laid-out train set right
now. It raced round and round – stopping at a little
station, going through a tunnel, chugging past little
waving model people and miniature houses, and it was
all perfect and somehow sunny. Nothing ever changed.
No one got on or off, but the train just raced round and
round this perfect afternoon.

It was just what she needed. She caught herself
checking her phone again. Of course she hadn't missed
a call. Or even a text. Just a text would have been OK.
Even if it said something bad. She turned back to the
train. It gave a tinny little whistle and she grinned. She
was cheered up.

The thing is, it wasn't a great day. Now Sunday – that had been a great night. She hadn't even been that drunk when she'd met him, and he was lovely and she'd skipped lectures on Monday and he'd taken her out for lunch at a café, and he had promised he'd call.

And it was now Thursday and not a peep. Of course, she was a big girl and these things no longer really hurt. She just got annoyed at how excited she got. Every time she sensed something starting, it was like things were painted in a glossy new colour and she got all giggly.

Plus she was in the middle of another essay crisis, and she really could have done with that 11 o'clock lecture on Monday morning. She'd borrowed Jessica's notes, but they'd told her nothing other than that she'd missed a really useful lecture. And so had Jess, seemingly. Oh well, she'd muddle through. A walk across the bridge, some hot dogs from Ikea, and then she'd sneak a pot of coffee into the library and spend an evening surrounded by books.

Maybe she'd find Tess as well. Tess, who'd been mocking her all week. 'So, when do we meet him? What's he like? Has he got you a ring yet? I bet he's got you a ring.' She knew Tess would be cruel but also more than happy to come along to the library. New Year's Resolution: *Get friends who actually like me more.*

The lights flickered in the store, and, for an instant, the train juddered in its perpetual glide around the track. Coming back to life, she wandered off around the toy shop. Down a nearby aisle, she saw a proud father trying out a computer game with his 8-year-old yelling on, unimpressed. She could see that the dad was half letting himself be led, half annoyed that he wasn't better at the game. 'No, Dad – you can use the red things. But if you don't let go of them quickly, then... you see. You're stupid, Dad.'

Nina decided that the word 'stupid' never sounded more devastating than when uttered in a thick Welsh accent. She smiled, and, just for an instant, the dad smiled at her too. And then, with a tiny wink, he turned back to the game, frowning in concentration while his son looked on.

Nina moved down the aisle, heading towards some weird kind of gothicky dolls. A grandmother was squinting down disapprovingly while a tiny girl in dungarees and bunches pointed critically at each one. 'Now, Nan,' she was saying, 'that one's Sister Slay – she comes with a choice of undertaker's outfit or butcher's apron. It's real good.'

'Yes, dear,' replied the old lady uncertainly, nervously tucking her hair under her woollen hat. 'I'm quite sure it's very nice. I had ever such a lovely teddy...'

The child ignored her, plucking another of the dolls off the shelf and shaking it. It made a screaming noise.

The lights flickered again, the train juddered, and Nina heard rain beating down on the concrete ceiling. Most people seemed unaffected, but there was a disappointed yell from the dad up the aisle – evidently his computer game had reset itself.

Nina mooched on, aware that the staff were calling closing time. She toyed with buying an inflatable slide, but dreaded to think how she'd inflate it, let alone fit it in her poky college room. Which reminded her that she was supposed to be flat-hunting. And that just depressed her even more.

When she'd first turned up in Cardiff, she wouldn't have been able to rent a studio flat out beyond Ikea. When she'd first started looking around, Cardiff estate agents had sneered before putting her on the waiting list for something behind Cathays Lidl with a combi boiler over the mouldy sink. Now she'd walk into their empty offices, windows crammed full of empty houses, and they'd smile and smile and smile. Things were so bad, they'd probably let her rent somewhere in SkyPoint, which was just mad when you thought about it. Which was why she was putting it off. She didn't like it when things weren't real.

The lights in the shop stuttered a further time, and the tannoy called out lazily, 'It's 8 o'clock, and the store is now closed. Please make your way promptly to the checkout with your purchases.' A handful of bored staff stood behind the tills, lopsided smiles on their faces as they urged everyone to go home.

Behind her, Nina could hear the grandmother saying firmly, 'Well, Anita, if you can't decide this time, I'm sure we can come back another day,' to outraged squeals.

Nina slotted a box back onto a shelf, and wandered to the exit. If it was starting to rain, then she wanted to get home before she got soaked. As she stepped towards the automatic door, it sliced open, and two figures marched in, both of them in fancy dress.

Nina paused, watching them. He was in army uniform, and looked very familiar. The woman appeared to be Jane Austen or something. Only she couldn't remember any Jane Austen character carrying a gun. Not even in *Sense and Sensibility*.

They swept past her, the man waving his phone up and down self-importantly. 'There's no sign of it,' he yelled to the woman.

She shrugged. 'You're just being impatient.'

'And you're still drunk.'

She barked at him with bitter laughter and hoisted the giant toy rocket launcher onto her shoulder.

Nina watched them, fascinated. This had all the makings of a top-class row. They were oblivious to the staff member heading towards them until she was standing next to them.

'We're closed,' the checkout woman growled. 'Please make your way to the nearest exit.'

'Hi!' beamed the man. 'We're just looking. Honestly – won't be a minute. Lego castle for our youngster, Ianto. We'll be in and out in a second.' And he widened the grin.

The woman was impassive and folded her arms. 'We're closed.'

Jane Austen glared at her, and belched slightly. 'Captain, I don't have time for shopkeepers,' she sighed and strode off down the aisle, looking for all the world as though she expected it to attack her.

The man shrugged helplessly, and lowered his voice conspiratorially. 'The missus – well, she's an unbearable cow at the best of times and a mean drunk. I'll just humour her and we'll be out from under your toes in a jiffy.' He paused and looked the woman up and down slowly. 'Not that I'm in a hurry.' And he grinned, a big cheesy grin.

Nina was horrified to see the checkout woman blush. Not only was Captain Cheese total sleaze – making a pass while out shopping with his wife for their kid, but he was just so… unreal. Convinced she'd seen him before, Nina carried on watching.

And then she noticed something. The kid and his dad were standing patiently by the automatic doors. Clearly, the staff had locked them. Someone slouched over from one of the tills, and reached out with a key to let them out into the dark. But the doors didn't budge. The kid from the tills kicked the door and then tried sliding it manually.

The noise alerted Captain Cheese. He glanced over, his face fell and he yelled: 'No! Leave the door. It'll—'

Nina never knew what 'it'll' meant. Instead, she watched, surprised and alarmed, as the door slid apart just slightly, and the night poured in, rolling over the screaming man.

The dad leapt back, dragging his son with him. There were cries. As Nina watched, Cheese swept forward, barking into his wristwatch. Jane Austen came thundering down the aisle.

'No! Down!' yelled Cheese.

Nina threw herself onto the floor and realised that the woman's rocket launcher was actually real. Or at least, it fired. But it didn't go off. It just vanished into the strange, shimmering black lump of night with a wet plop and was gone.

Captain Cheese and Jane Austen raced over to the door and dragged it shut, Jane using the butt of her gun to squeeze the black thing back out as the man slid the door shut. They both collapsed against it, panting with exhaustion. They glared at each other with a mixture of relief and fury, and then turned to face the small handful of shocked shoppers and staff.

'You will remain calm!' barked Jane Austen. 'There is nothing to concern you. Please continue to purchase your haberdashery without another thought.' The man winced. 'Kindly move away from this porch while my colleague and I contain the situation.'

'What bloody situation?' screamed the manager who'd confronted them earlier. 'And where's Colin?'

'Dead,' Jane Austen pointed at the floor. 'His name badge is there if you're interested.'

Captain Cheese looked pained. 'Hey!' he said, with a desperate air of bonhomie. 'There's a situation. But we can probably get through this together.'

The girl who was with her grandmother started to cry.

'Is it aliens?' the young boy asked, eyes wide.

Captain Cheese knelt down. 'Might be. Might be, you know. Ever met one before?'

The boy shook his head, seriously.

'Well, they're not all bad. But this one is. If it is an alien.'

Jane Austen snorted. 'Of course it's an alien, you posturing oaf.' She gestured to the back of the store and squinted at the manager's name badge. 'You! Janice – is there a secure room backstairs?'

'Well, there's the staff room but we're not allowed to let—'

'That door is not going to hold for long.' Jane Austen huffed with disdain. 'Just take them to it, and do it now.'

'… health and safety,' finished Janice, weakly.

Jane Austen turned to Captain Cheese and said, much to Nina's surprise, 'Are all the people of this time so feeble? I blame central heating, I really do.'

So, there they all were in the staff room. Nina, Anita and her gran, the young boy and his dad, and, over in a corner, quacking like mother and her ducklings, was Janice the manager and the half-dozen staff. They clearly resented the intrusion, but Nina didn't think they had that much to crow about. The staff room was a corner of breeze blocks, with some laminated notices, a yellowing plastic kettle and some battle-weary pieces of office furniture.

Captain Cheese pulled a blind over the small window set into the door then surveyed the room sharply. 'Good,'

98

he said. His eyes were drawn by an air vent at ground level. It was rattling slightly. 'Bad,' he said. 'It'll try and get through that.' He pushed a sofa across the vent.

'Thank you, dear,' sighed Gran, and sat down, looking oddly complacent.

'Right,' said Captain Cheese. A silence had settled over the room, and everyone was staring at him. Clearly expecting an explanation. Even Jane Austen.

Oh, thought Nina, *this'll be good.*

'Right,' said Captain Cheese again.

Janice the manager leapt into the silence. 'Well, my mobile isn't working. What is going on?'

Cheese breathed in. 'So, your toy shop is surrounded by a giant alien parasite intent on consuming everything inside it. Which will be your stock, and then you. But it's not picky. We're here to stop that.'

'And you are?' asked Gran sharply.

Janice glanced at her. Clearly she'd wanted to say that.

Cheese looked as though he was about to tell them, but was silenced by a glare from Jane Austen, who stepped forward.

You know what, thought Nina, *I'm going out on a limb. They're not married – they work together. And hate each other. In fancy dress. Neat.*

Jane Austen looked around the room, freezing any opposition with a tight smile. 'So. We are authorised to contain extraterrestrial menace. Help is on the way. Remain here. Stay calm. You may rely on us to deal with the situation.'

'My colleague has a very big gun,' said Cheese with a grin.

In the distance came the groaning tinkle of the entry doors being forced open.

'Oh dear,' tutted Jane Austen, swaying slightly. 'As he said. Stay here. Remain calm. Captain, we have work to do.' And, priming her rocket launcher, she swept out.

The Captain stood on the threshold for an instant and looked apologetic. With his voice lowered he whispered, 'Seriously, we're good at this. And she means well. You'll be fine. Don't open the door to anything with tentacles.' And then, with a large grin and a wink, he vanished.

For a minute, there was an uncomfortable silence. And then Janice tried to reassert her authority.

You're a nasty piece of work, thought Nina, watching Janice bully her staff. *How come someone so joyless gets to run a toy shop? Still, at least she's doing something reasonably harmless. Not in charge of cancer research or anything.*

Janice picked up the landline, intent on reaching the outside world and normality. She pushed a few buttons and then put the handset down. Almost sadly.

'Well,' she said. 'We're cut off. Does anyone have a mobile signal?'

Everyone shook their heads. Even Anita had a phone, Nina noticed. It was pink and had buttons. Bless. Nina stared at her own. It said 'Emergency Calls Only' which turned out to be a bit of a lie. She wondered about sending a text, and who she'd send it to, and what it would say.

She started picking out a few keys, figuring she could just keep pressing Send and maybe it would go through. 'Am in toy shop eaten by alien. Byeeeee'? 'Mum, I'm on BBC News'? Although Nina's mum had never sent or received a text message. She had her mobile glued to her ear like a radio, but she never got into 'the writing side of things', as she put it. Would she be startled when it suddenly seemed her phone was talking to her? She shrugged. *I am avoiding thinking about what's going on. Should I be more scared?*

If little Anita was sullenly quiet, the young boy wasn't. Impatiently swinging his legs backwards and forwards he started to ask his dad questions to which he couldn't possibly know the answer in a piercing whine.

Dad was clearly a bit freaked by the whole situation, but then, who wouldn't be? All he could do was reply, 'I dunno, Scott,' or other variants.

Scott retreated to comforting ground. 'Dad,' he asked, 'have you got any chocolate?'

Again, Dad shook his head, miserable at having failed even this test.

'Hey,' said Nina, rootling around in her shoulder bag, and pulling out a large slab of chocolate. 'I got this at the newsagents. You know how it is,' she was babbling, 'you buy a newspaper, they throw sweets at you.' She handed it over, and, noticing the avaricious eyes of Anita, said sweetly to the room, 'There's plenty – help yourselves, everyone.'

With the sharing of little squares of not very nice chocolate, everyone bonded a little. Gran piped up from the sofa, 'Janice, dear, why don't you make us all a lovely cup of tea?'

Janice, mouth full of three squares of chocolate, looked sharply at the kettle, the little stack of plastic cups and the pathetic pile of teabags in a chipped old mug and honestly, thoroughly, visibly wished they weren't there, but instead squeezed out a watery smile. 'It's not usual procedure,' she said, her voice a little sticky with chocolate, 'But why not, eh?' She performed an ugly swallow, like a snake devouring an egg. 'Kevin, put the kettle on for the customers, why don't you?'

Nina slouched back against the wall and listened to the sounds of gunfire. *Odd day,* she thought.

The Vam poured into the building exultantly. 'This is the feast of the Vam!' it roared to itself. It was a complicated biological cry that echoed through every one of its cells, a thrill at a genetic level that spurred it on, forcing it to divide and multiply, to surge and devour. The Vam was alive. The Vam was filled with delight.

(The Vam was also vaguely aware that the last time it had uttered this cry had been as it wrapped itself around an entire solar system, squeezing planets into the sun until they'd popped like a fistful of songbirds. But here it was, squeezing into an ugly warehouse next to a tile factory off the Penarth Road. Ah well. It was aware of the concept of bathos. Those had been the glory days. And there would be new glory days ahead. But first, the feast of the Vam!)

This feast was not without interest. For the first time it was aware of resistance. The Vam had always treated resistance like a spice. It enjoyed it. The stronger the better, the greater the savour. It thrilled to sense that the doomed creatures of this planet knew it was a threat and were marshalling their puny failures of weapons against it. This was, it knew, just the first wave. A couple of soldiers armed with projectile weapons. Soon they would be replaced with battalions, with armies, with fearsome engines of death, with desperate final measures, as entire continents were destroyed in the futile hope of halting the progress of the Vam. But Ha! Ha! You cannot stop the Vam. The Vam is a universal force. The Vam is a scientific process. The Vam surges and devours!

That said, the Vam possessed a mild curiosity. It sensed a captive audience, and reached out to learn a little more.

Jack and Agnes thundered down the aisle as shelves toppled around them like dominoes. They hurled themselves behind a girder as a sea of sundered metal and toys spilled around them. Agnes leaned around the corner and fired off another rocket into the giant, black mass that poured relentlessly into the building.

Agnes watched the trail of the rocket as it soared through the air and vanished into the blackness with a quiet little plop. There was no explosion. Just a tiny little *phut* and a little puff of air. That was it. As there hadn't been on any of the previous times before.

'I'm sure you're wearing it down,' said Jack drily.

Agnes ignored him, reloading her weapon. 'As long as I have rockets, it is my duty to this country to attempt to contain this monstrosity.'

'It's not going to work,' said Jack.

'It is important to try.' Agnes fired off another missile, her posture barely shifting under the kickback. 'The Empire wasn't built by people just rolling over. You've always been only too eager to,' she finished sourly.

'Agnes,' Jack tried a reasonable tone. 'It's not going to work. That creature is too big. We've got to find a way to rescue those people and get out. We'll find a solution. We lose this battle, but we win the war.'

Agnes fished around in her shoulder holster and sighed. 'I have only three pieces of ordnance left. What do you suggest?'

The kickback from the gun knocked Jack off his skates and onto the blood-soaked floor of the roller-discotheque. In the distance, over the twitching headless corpses, he could see Agnes gliding past, firing shots into the dancers, her exultant face flashing with reflections from the glitterball.

'Captain Jack Harkness!' she bellowed. 'Get off your fundament!' And then, with a whoop, she was away.

Murmuring hatefully, Jack tried to stand up, the roller skates shooting away from him, and leaving him scrabbling like a kitten on polished lino.

Whatever Agnes had said, they definitely were not blending in.

'Harkness!' she yelled again.

'I. Am. Trying,' growled Jack, pitching painfully onto his shoulder. He'd never got the hang of roller skates.

'No, Harkness, look out!' somehow Agnes's warning was tinged with exasperation.

Jack twisted over awkwardly, managing to neatly shatter the chin off an attacker with a flailing skate. The zombie staggered back, blood spurting through a cloud of dry ice.

Jack fired his gun and watched the corpse fall to the floor.

Agnes swished past, executed a neat turn, stopped on point, and offered him her hand.

'Honestly, Harkness. When I was a child, one was skating on the Thames before mounting one's first pony.'

'I've never mounted a pony,' muttered Jack.

'Well, we must be thankful for small mercies,' said Agnes, propelling him neatly to the sidelines. 'You can provide covering fire from the barriers.'

'Are these really zombies?' Jack had never really believed in the Undead.

Agnes shook her head. 'Of course not. These poor unfortunates are probably just the victims of a lethal space plague.'

'Uh-huh.' Jack leaned against a thumping speaker and fired off a shot, sending a hot-panted attacker reeling back. 'Is that a technical term?'

Agnes smiled tightly. 'I am sure that space medicine has advanced since my day. I leave you to fill in the details.'

And she soared across the floor in a graceful arc towards a huddled clutch of the living. 'Goodness!' she gasped to Jack. 'In these skirts I must look like one of the Georgian State Dancers.'

And then one of the Undead dropped on her from the lighting rig. Agnes howled and fell to the floor, trying to keep its drooling teeth from her neck. Her gun had fallen from her.

'Harkness!' she cried, gasping with pain as a talon raked across her arm.

Jack let go of the railing, and wobbled unsteadily to her rescue.

'I knew we should never have come to Sweden,' said Agnes.

It was later. The lights had come on in the roller discotheque. Grim-suited men in uniform were dragging sequined corpses from the floor and collecting up various body parts. Occasionally one of them would shoot an angry glance at the figure in military uniform crouched over a woman in elaborately old-fashioned skirts, sat awkwardly on an orange plastic chair.

Jack was leaning over Agnes, wiping down her arm with iodine. She winced, and looked up at him. 'You're enjoying this, aren't you, Captain?'

He smiled, just slightly. 'Mostly, I'm waiting to see if the infection takes hold.'

'Ah,' said Agnes quietly. 'Yes. I rather fear you'll enjoy shooting me in the head.'

Jack shrugged. 'I'm fairly sure it's my turn. Scared?'

Agnes paused for a second before replying.

'Well, it certainly isn't the plan. Mind you, this century isn't exactly what I was expecting.'

'That's Torchwood for you,' said Jack.

'Indeed,' said Agnes. 'And you do hang around it a lot, if I may say. I expected you would be long gone. Instead you keep turning up like a bad penny.'

'I guess I'm just looking for a home,' Jack replied.

'And is Torchwood really your home?'

Jack shrugged. 'Sometimes, I think so. Sometimes not. And then I'll go travelling for a bit. Or do something totally different. I had a brief spell in life insurance.' He caught Agnes's glance. 'Yeah, I know. Didn't last long. Then there was the burger bar on Bondi Beach. That was fun. But I always come back to Torchwood.'

'Well, I'm sure we're all very grateful,' said Agnes tightly.

Jack smiled at her, surprisingly fondly. 'We have our moments, you know.'

Agnes looked at him. 'And whatever do you mean by that, Captain Harkness?'

Jack grinned. 'You, me, a disco, the Undead, two guns, and one sense of balance. There aren't many people I can do this kind of thing with.'

Agnes laughed a little. 'I suppose that's true.'

'And, seriously, the twentieth century is proving pretty eventful,' he told her. 'You're actually seeing some of the more interesting corners of it.'

Agnes nodded. 'It's just so uncertain. I never know what I'll see when I wake up. I've a younger sister... I had a younger sister. Tilly. I tried to look her up when I first awoke. But by then... I don't know. I couldn't find her. I had so much to tell her. I could always tell her anything. And she was gone. That was a shock. And that was a couple of weeks ago. Mama. Papa. Tilly. Everything I knew is just history. And now my one remaining link to the past...'

'Me?' said Jack with a rueful smile.

Agnes frowned. 'Well, yes, there is you, I suppose.'

Jack chuckled. 'Faint praise indeed, Miss Havisham. We will

have to get used to each other. At this rate, you'll be around another thousand years.'

Agnes snorted, nearly causing a policeman to drop the corpse he was carrying. 'Familiarity breeds contempt, Harkness.' She giggled. 'Jack.'

'Oh, it does, Agnes, it does indeed.' Jack squeezed her shoulder and smiled.

And then he kissed her.

Captain Jack Harkness sat alone in the empty roller disco, nursing a fractured jaw. He stood carefully, and rolled towards the exit in search of his boots. Down the road, somewhere, he knew Abba were in concert. And he'd be able to get a ticket off of Agnetha. Or was it Bjorn? One of the blondes, anyway. He looked up at the lone glitterball that still sparkled as it turned, and then he walked out the door.

Gran, slumbering on the sofa, woke suddenly and looked around. Anita handed her a beaker of tea, which she took, blinking with momentary confusion and then a weak smile.

Nina wandered over to the staff-room door, where Janice was peering through the slats in the blind. Under her breath she was saying, 'Well, our insurance is covered for flood. This is a mud slide. I'm fairly certain, oh yes, that we're covered for mud.'

Through the slits, Nina could see the giant black thing flinging steel racks around like paper darts. The noise was terrific, not helped by the way the walls of the building were making a remarkable noise. It was, she figured, the sound of concrete being squeezed.

Occasionally, she'd see two figures darting between aisles, somehow keeping on fighting – both the creature and each other. It was so oddly, reassuringly human that she felt, against all the odds, a little bit of hope.

There we go, Nina Rogers, she thought. *You're probably going to be eaten by a giant alien blob, but you're still feeling all upbeat. That's nice.*

'Goodness,' said Gran, sitting up. 'Are those two having any luck out there?'

'No,' sighed Janice. She was watching as a whole set of swings and trampolines flew past.

'Do we know anything about them, dear? I just think it's important to know what organisation they represent, don't you?'

There was a muttering of agreement.

Irritated, Gran pressed on. 'But does anyone know who those people are? What authority they have?'

Everyone shook their heads.

'We don't know who they are, Nan,' said Anita, dolefully.

'They're superheroes,' put in young Scott, hopefully.

'Oh, I see,' said Gran quietly. 'That's nice.'

'I'm going to take a sample,' said Jack, grinning. 'Cover me.'

Agnes ducked as a volley of mountain bikes flew over their heads and clattered into the walls.

'At least if we can learn something from all this…'

Agnes opened her mouth to protest, but then nodded. 'It's the first sensible thing you've said today. You have fifteen seconds.' She raised her rocket launcher and, instead of directing it at the creature, fired it at a row of computers. The resulting explosion scattered clouds of razor shrapnel towards the creature.

Jack threw an arm across his face and vanished into the maelstrom.

'I don't believe it,' groaned Janice. 'They're firing at the stock.'

'Yes, dear,' tutted Gran sympathetically. 'But who would normally be called at such an emergency?'

Dad looked up. 'My brother's a fireman,' he said. 'He's seen a fair few remarkable things these last couple of years. But I don't think…'

'The army,' said Anita suddenly, certainly. 'Soldiers would be good at this.'

Scott nodded, excited. 'With their tanks and their nuclear weapons and their harrier jump jets.'

'That's the air force!' cried out Anita, happy and excited.

'I see,' said Gran, shifting slightly on the sofa. 'But what if they weren't enough? What then? Who would help us then?'

Jack was pressed underneath a checkout counter. Flapping around him was the burning hail of what had once been a bouncy Princess castle. He watched as the plastic fragments slapped into the alien creature and were instantly absorbed.

The mass pressed up against the formica and steel of the checkout, and Jack knew he only had seconds left. Hurriedly, he grabbed a carrier bag from the counter and reached out to scoop a sample, like a dog owner picking up a turd. And then he remembered that the alien ate plastic and dropped the bag hurriedly. He looked around again, patting his pockets without luck. He knew that Torchwood had bonded polycarbide bags that could hold almost anything. Failing that were portable force-field containers. But he didn't have any on him. Instead he made do with a steel cash box, hoping that the steel would hold it. He reached out and snapped the box shut, and then, as the checkout splintered around him, he ran, ducking slightly as a rocket soared over his head and thudded wetly into the shivering black blob.

The Vam had sensed the little man. It knew he wanted a sample. And the Vam felt generous. Let these humans find out what they were up against. After all, it was doing exactly the same.

'I wonder what they're doing,' said Gran.

Anita, perched on a desk, beckoned her over. 'Come and have a look.'

Gran shook her head. 'I don't think so, dear. I'm quite comfortable here. Just tell me what they're up to.'

'Cowering,' said Janice, dismissively.

'Oh,' said Gran. 'I expect they'll die in a minute.'

Anita looked at her in shock. 'Nan!' she wailed.

Gran patted her hand. 'Oh, hush,' she said. 'They're clearly outclassed. They've just got guns. It'll all be over quite quickly.'

Jack joined Agnes underneath the burning remains of the train set.

All around them the building was shuddering, giant corrugated sheets splintering down as the creature dripped in around them.

'Retreat?' suggested Agnes.

'Oh yeah,' agreed Jack.

'Shall we join the others?' Agnes loosed off the last rocket and threw aside the spent gun. She hoisted up her crinolines. 'Let's strike out!'

'Yeah. They can make us a cup of tea,' said Jack and raced after her.

Behind them, the store shattered in a rain of concrete and steel.

Agnes and Jack pelted through the door of the staff room, slamming it somewhat pointlessly behind them. They stood there, panting for a few seconds and then guiltily met the gazes of the other people in the room. Hope had been replaced by a look of fear and betrayal. They'd swept in, they'd assumed authority, and, as far as anyone could see, they hadn't achieved much.

Nina almost felt sorry for them. What could they really expect – two people up against a big devouring blob?

Jack flashed a weak smile. 'It's honestly better than it looks, folks. Our top priority now is getting you out.'

'Oh, really,' said Gran. 'And how are you going to manage that? You're surrounded.'

Jack's smile didn't even flicker. 'Not completely surrounded, ma'am,' he said.

His confidence was undermined by the rattling, roaring devastation of the rest of the building falling in and tumbling towards them like a lost game of Jenga.

'Down!' roared Agnes, snatching Janice and Nina to the floor.

Debris smashed in through the glass of the staff room door, spreading dust and splinters everywhere.

For a few seconds there was silence, and then the crying began. Not, noticed Nina, from the kids. Anita and Scott were both tremblingly silent. But Janice had started to sob uncontrollably. One of her staff was trying to comfort her, with the ease of someone trying to pat a live electrical cable.

Jack and Agnes stood up, dusting themselves off.

'Not long now,' said Gran. She'd retained her seat on the sofa, even though she was now coated with dust.

Jack looked at her. 'There's still time,' he said. 'There's still hope.'

Gran shook her head, and smiled at him sadly. 'No, there isn't. And tell me, please, what happens next? After you, who will come? The army? And when that army is defeated, who will then arrive? Who then will come to die?'

Jack's gaze hardened. But it was Agnes who spoke. 'People will come. And they will try. And they will die, if necessary. But they will try. Because that creature is evil. It is alien. It is wrong. It must be fought. If necessary to the last man, woman and child.'

'I see,' said Gran, nodding. 'That's nice to know. Thank you.'

'But it's not over yet,' vowed Jack.

'Yes it is, dear,' said Gran. 'This is the feast of the Vam. Goodbye.'

And the Vam surged up and out of Gran, pouring through the air vent, the sofa, and streaming in wild tentacles through the little old lady's ruptured body.

At precisely the same time the outer walls of the staff room gave in, pouring bricks and concrete and steel and dust down into the tiny room.

X

REAPING
THE WHIRLWIND

In which Mrs Cooper encounters the gentlemen of the press,
and Miss Havisham prevails against the government of nations

As the building fell in around them a very neat, very square hole snicked open in the floor.

'Ianto!' cried Jack with relief, scooping up a screaming Anita, and ushering everyone down the hole. As concrete bricks thundered down around her, Agnes took one last, grim look around, before fixing on the flopping wet puppet of the old woman. And, just for a second, she looked worried. And then she jumped into the tunnel.

Outside, Ianto and Gwen were herding the survivors into ambulances.

To Jack's eyes, the scene was startling. Squatting over the entire building was a vast black mass, as rich and sticky as toffee. It seemed to roar, but that was simply the sound of the girders rent beneath it.

It was surrounded by police cars and ambulances; there was even a fire engine, of all things, hosing it down.

Several camera crews filmed the proceedings under the shifting blue lights of the sirens.

For a second, Jack just took in the absurdity of the scene – after all these days of worry, the end of the world was happening, and the Apocalypse wasn't a sky of fire and a boiling sea with hordes of hellspawn tearing through a rain of burning coals – instead it began with the municipal authorities hosing down a giant bin liner. He smiled, and idly checked out a passing fireman.

Ianto came running up to him, and, making sure that Agnes wasn't looking, hugged him. Jack, careless, seized his cheeks and kissed him. Ianto squirmed away uneasily. 'Not on duty, Captain,' he whispered.

'Tut,' said Jack fondly as Ianto straightened his tie. 'Thank you.'

Ianto looked bashful. 'I'm sorry it took so long. It was almost impossible to get a fix on you through that… thing. We tried digging the tunnel through it, but the cutting equipment wouldn't touch it. It's like the thing's got a force field. So I had to go down.'

Jack started to say something.

'You did well, Mr Jones,' said Agnes. She'd materialised behind them almost silently and stood there, actually smiling as she picked dirt from her gloves. 'A most timely rescue.' She grinned at him and patted him on the shoulder.

Ianto grew visibly.

She then turned to survey the mayhem around them. 'Goodness me,' she sighed. 'What a mess.'

'All my fault?' asked Jack.

'Oh yes,' said Agnes with the tone of an eternally patient, eternally disappointed teacher. 'But we shall have to see what we can do. Mrs Cooper!'

Gwen broke away from complicated discussions with three policemen, a fire sergeant and a traffic warden and came running over. She looked stressed, but thoroughly in charge.

Agnes looked around her and drew herself up. 'We shall have to have a quick field conference everyone. Now, we've fallen at the first gate and clearly the anticipated alien threat has not been prevented. Secondly, we have been unable to contain the situation without the help of civil authorities. Thirdly, those oiks over there savour of Her Majesty's Press, so we can assume that public knowledge of this alien menace will hit the streets within days. And, fourthly and finally, I rather fear we shall be spared public disgrace, as, given that creature's exponential rate of growth, I predict that it will have spread all the way to Bedfordshire by next week and the continent in a fortnight. The fate of the world, is, very literally, in our hands.' Agnes beamed and then cocked an eyebrow at Jack. 'And I believe you said, only a short while ago, "Crisis? What crisis?" Shame on you, Harkness.'

'So what do we do?' said Gwen, sensing Jack's rigid frame.

Agnes placed her hands on her hips and waved away an approaching camera crew. 'Mrs Cooper, please continue the excellent civil liaison work that you've been

117

undertaking. The rest of us have a sample of that creature which we shall examine in the Hub. We'll be back as soon as we can.'

Back at the Hub, Agnes, Jack and Ianto stared at the open cash box. Inside, the fragment of the Vam had expanded to fill the tin, which was starting to rattle slightly. Already the sides of the tin were melting. They'd rapidly transferred it to a containment field.

Jack set up a chemical analysis while Agnes demanded an inventory of weapons from Ianto. She was hoping there was something somewhere in their armoury. She scanned down the clipboard Ianto had presented her with. 'It's a shame we don't have a giant containment-field generator,' she tutted, running a finger down the list.

'Don't look at me,' Jack shouted over. 'There's not much call these days to contain something the size of a small village.'

As she flung herself through the gap, the air behind her lit up a bright, crackling blue and a wave of heat rushed past her. She landed awkwardly on the ground.

A hand reached down to help her up, but she ignored it.

'I should have expected to find you here,' she said.

Jack grinned. 'We've contained it.' He gestured to the troops behind him operating the field barriers. 'A little something I brought back from Torchwood India about ten years ago. Seems to be doing the trick.'

Agnes carefully smoothed down her hopelessly creased skirts.

'An appearance at the last minute, I see, Harkness. If you had been earlier, we might very well have saved some of the facility.'

Jack demurred. 'We've contained the threat. And, bonus, we got you out alive. Another second and you'd have been sealed on the other side of that force wall for ever.' He sighed.

Agnes glared at him. 'Not for ever, Harkness. I believe those shields will only hold back the threat for five thousand years. A postponement, not a defeat.'

Jack grinned. 'Well then, after our time, I hope.'

Agnes paused before replying. 'Sadly unlikely, Harkness. When those walls come down, I shall be waiting. And so, I fear, shall you.'

Jack smiled, 'Like a bad penny, ma'am,' he said.

And this time, when he offered her his hand, she took it.

Agnes looked up. 'Ah yes,' she said crisply, 'I remember. You only just got out of there alive, didn't you, Harkness? I trust that the barriers around that place are still working? We could dismantle them, I suppose, but then that would just unleash… no.'

'I don't think a force field would work anyway,' sighed Jack. The light blue field around the blob had started to spark and crackle alarmingly. 'That creature is drawing energy off of it. Very efficiently. Our sample could very well become another of those things.'

Agnes glanced sharply at the shuddering mass. 'I do so hate something I can't shoot. What does the analysis suggest?'

Jack tapped a screen. 'Oh,' he said.

At exactly the same time, the mass quivered, shook and died.

'A chemical spill?' asked the man from BBC News.

'Oh yes,' said Gwen.

'It's the size of a football pitch.'

'It's a big chemical spill.'

'And appears to be moving.'

'Spilling. It's what spills do.'

He looked at her, boiling with frustration, and then turned on his heel and stormed off to shout at his camera crew. Gwen stood her ground, checking that the broadcast damper in the SUV was still working. Good. Something the size of that thing would only cause a national panic.

She was so sodding tired and not a little drunk. It had been quite a day, and looked like getting a whole lot worse. Despite what Agnes had said, they'd worked so hard to stop something like this happening. As soon as those coffins had turned up, Jack had said they were trouble. But this was getting off the scale – rapidly and horribly.

Her phone chirruped again. She sighed and answered it. It was, no doubt, someone else's boss's boss's boss angrily demanding an explanation he could give his boss. She breathed in, said to herself very quietly, 'This is not my fault.' Then she took the call.

Trying to coordinate a civil response was proving tricky. The police had been easy – keeping people away, stopping traffic – all fairly easy, and no worse than sealing off St Mary Street from the innocent on a Saturday night. Getting those shop people off to hospital had got rid of a few ambulance crews, but more kept turning up, as though waiting hopefully for casualties. The firemen had, eventually, been persuaded to stop spraying the blob with water – all that was doing was making the ground slippery.

The firemen had sent a special chemical spills team out, who strode around wearing white protective suits, but at least they backed up her cover story.

Someone had set up floodlights, which gave passers-by a jolly lovely view. It wasn't going to be long before a camera crew set themselves up outside Gwen's damping field and the whole thing went global.

Perfect, she thought.

She was now tentatively explaining to a nice man from the Assembly that, no, Cardiff didn't need evacuating, and no, reports he'd heard of a nuclear weapon or terrorist strike were rashly ill-informed. 'It's just a big black blob. It's eating things. We just need to keep everyone out of its way while we work out what to do with it,' she explained, endlessly patient. 'We're Torchwood. This is why we're here. This is what we do,' she said calmly and with total authority.

Sod it. She called Rhys. 'You watching the news?'

'No!' he laughed back. 'Why would I? There's a *Two Pints* marathon on BBC Three. What is it, love?' A slightly forced tone. 'World finally ending, is it?'

'Yeah,' said Gwen.

'Want to talk about it?'

'Not really.'

'Fine.' In the background, Gwen could just hear him turning down the pre-recorded laughter of a studio audience and a little bit of applause. She imagined him, spread out in the flat, taking up both his and her halves of the sofa, bottle of beer resting on the floor. He'd probably made lasagne. Yeah, that'd be nice.

'Lasagne's in the oven,' he said. 'You gonna be long?'

'Dunno,' she sighed. 'Like I said, world ending.'

'Well, just try and pop in before it's all over.'

'I love you,' she said, and got back to being patronised by someone from the Welsh Natural Disasters Prevention Agency who had a) got her number from somewhere, and b) not realised that this wasn't a natural disaster or that the horse had already bolted and that yelling about a nice new stable door wasn't going to do much good. Lovely, she thought – this is let's bollock Gwen Cooper day. If I'd wanted that, I'd have gone and been a traffic warden. The nice thing about Torchwood was that you could always be sure that you could ring round and get all the authorities on your side. The disadvantage was that this meant they all had your phone number, and had a nasty habit of ringing you up at the first sign of trouble. Sometimes, she just wished they'd all sod off.

Behind her, the big black blob, glistening under all that water, reached out casually and consumed a fire engine.

***

122

The Vam exulted. These creatures knew about it and they feared it. That was the true feast of the Vam. The sheer joy of what it was doing fuelled its expansion, and it swelled and twisted, sucking the very last of the toy shop into itself and swelling out. It realised it was surrounded – the forces of the locals making a first doomed attempt at containment, with all their little vehicles, or, as the Vam thought of them, snacks.

It considered what to do next, idly popping out a few thousand eyes to watch the conflagration beneath. Obviously it was going to expand, to surge and devour, but in which direction? It could sense a large cluster of… suburban dwellings on the other side of the road. The crowd which was currently watching it, learning to fear and curse the name of the Vam, why, they had streamed from them in curiosity. The Vam could just extend out a little way and take them with very, very little effort.

So it did.

'Get back!' screamed Gwen. Everyone had been busy watching one side of the creature devouring the fire engine, but she'd noticed the back swell out and start to topple over onto the watching crowd. She grabbed a discarded loudhailer that the emergency services had been using to shout at each other and screamed into the crowd, 'Run!'

The crowd heard her, but stood frozen, staring at the surging mass.

A lone photographer ran forward, crouching down in

front of the monster. Horrified, Gwen screamed at him through the loudhailer. 'For Christ's sake get out of the way, you bloody idiot!'

The crowd's natural deference to someone in authority – perhaps mixed with their vague feeling that it wasn't all that usual to be sworn at through a loudhailer – prompted almost everyone to leg it. But the photographer stood his ground, trying to get the perfect shot. Which he did. And then the Vam ate him and then his camera.

A sticky black curtain poured down between Gwen and the crowd. She could see them running away, and that was all she needed to know.

Then the beast, as though sensing that she had warned its prey, splattered and oozed down on her.

Agnes looked up from the microscope. 'Fascinating. Complex hydrocarbons, elementary protein strains. This is like a primordial soup that was too lazy to bother evolving out of the swamps and just... became a self-regenerating organism.' She giggled. 'I suppose you're all rather used to the principles of Mr Darwin, but I must admit, I still find it all rather novel. Even when I'm confronted by marvels of creation that outclass anything offered by the Galapagos, I'm still...' She smiled. 'This is an extraordinary example of an efficient, lethal being.'

'It's petrol,' said Jack. 'It's petrol that thinks.'

'Actually,' muttered Ianto, 'strictly speaking, it's closer to diesel.'

'What?' Agnes looked at them both. 'And you really...?'

She stopped, frowning. 'If you'll excuse me, I just need to go and check something on your internet.'

'OK,' said Jack. 'While you do that, I'll just upload our results to a concerned colleague at UNIT. She's our unofficial scientific adviser – and she may be able to offer a slightly more complex analysis.'

Agnes waved a hand distractedly at him. She was already sat down at a terminal, pulling information out of it.

'Righto,' sighed Ianto. 'I'll make some tea, then.'

Gwen was still alive, marvellously. She wasn't quite so sure about everyone else around her, but the noise and the smell were extraordinary. It was like a gas station mixed with rotten trout. And it was everywhere.

She opened her eyes, and realised she was buried under bricks that were shifting as though some enormous weight was... Oh God. The thing was on top of her. The bricks ground and shifted as the black mass moved, and pressed down against her... and then suddenly went away.

Gwen, gagging, eyes watering from the stench, pulled herself gently up. She'd have liked to think she sprang up immediately, but it actually took her about two minutes before she plucked up the courage to move. Her body had just frozen with the sheer horror of it all.

She realised that all that had been on top of her was a tendril of the creature, which was shifting its shape, rolling out thick coils across the ground as it moved its bulk. She scrambled out from under the bricks and stood watching as it swept some abandoned cars towards itself. Ahead of her, she realised, were a few scattered policemen. She looked for a face she recognised in the crowd but couldn't see any. A camera crew had assembled by a toppled ambulance, trying to get a picture lit. Some firemen stood around in a desultory fashion. Behind her, she was aware, the crowd had re-formed.

Her phone rang. It said 'withheld', which promised yet another furious government official. She nerved herself for the inevitable.

As she took the call, she watched one of the firemen being hunted by a flapping tendril. It closed in on him, and he threw out a hand to defend himself. Instead, it latched on to his hand, and dragged him towards itself. Colleagues ran towards him, trying to free him from the tendril. Instead it flowed under him and snared them too, pulling in a leisurely, macabre tug of war towards itself. With shouts and yells, they braced themselves, pulling in a macho fashion, with some laughter and encouragement. But gradually they realised the hopelessness of their situation and just pulled back against the inevitable.

The crowd started to scream and cry. Some brave souls rushed up, and they too became ensnared, inching painfully towards the bulk of the monster.

Gwen switched off her phone mid-rant and just watched, horrified.

***

Agnes stood up from the terminal and crossed over to Jack. 'Did you send those findings on to your United Nations contact?'

'Yes,' said Jack. 'And they're very interested.'

'I bet they are,' snapped Agnes. 'You are to have no further communication with them.'

'What?' said Jack. 'But—'

'They've reached the same conclusions about this creature as I have myself. And they leak like a colander. In the last two minutes I have had offers of assistance from the Kremlin, from the Crown Prince of Saudi Arabia, and from the Oval Office. It is vitally important that we get back to that creature before anyone else does.'

There was nothing they could do. Onlookers stood by the sweating, crying chain of people, carefully not touching them, just watching, not meeting any of their desperate eyes.

Gwen ran up. 'What's your name?' she asked the first fireman.

'Ted,' he replied. 'I've caused all of this, haven't I?'

'No,' said Gwen. 'It's a trap, that's all.'

He strained, trying to lift a hand from the impossibly viscous mass that was oozing around his wrists and then he looked at her. 'Can you get my phone?' he pleaded.

Gwen reached out, and then stopped. 'I'm sorry,' she said. 'I daren't touch you.'

'Oh God,' he sobbed, and was dragged another step closer to the monster. 'I want to phone my girlfriend.'

'Sure,' said Gwen. 'Just tell me the number.'

He shook his head, tears streaming down his cheeks. 'That's the problem. I don't know. I can never remember it. I just want to speak to her.' He looked up at the shuddering mass, now so close to him, and he turned back to Gwen, his eyes as frightened as a child's. 'Oh God,' he breathed. 'I've not got long have I?' He slumped forward, the tendril jerking him even closer.

Gwen nearly reached out to him, but stopped herself. 'I'm sorry,' she said. 'But it's OK. Tell me her name – I can find the number out. The people I work for are very good.'

'Ianto?'

'Yes?'

'Can you get me a number for a Lorraine Leung?'

'Sure. Why?'

'It's important, that's all.'

Gwen held the mobile as close to the man as she dared.

'The mobile you are trying to reach is currently unavailable. Please call again later.'

The man just stood there, shaking all over, and was dragged even closer to the beast's shimmering surface.

As the SUV roared up the road, the sky around them darkened. The creature had raised itself up, almost blocking out the sun. It looked like a swollen cloud come to Earth.

Sat in the front seat, Agnes looked at it. And she smiled, slightly.

The fireman screamed as his hand touched the surface of the creature, flowing around and sucking him in.

Gwen stood, watching, crying. 'I'm sorry,' she shouted. 'Sorry!' She wanted to reach out, to touch him as he struggled, but she kept her hands by her sides. 'Sorry,' she said again.

Ted drew breath as his body vanished into the creature, his head twisting around to look at her. The black gel oozed around his face, pouring into his eyes and his nose. His mouth opened wide and screamed. And then the scream stopped, and Gwen was just staring at a wide-open mouth poking out of the shuddering black mass.

The mouth spoke. 'This is the feast of the Vam,' it said.

And then the fireman pulled the rest of the crowd in after him.

And Gwen Cooper stood and watched.

Agnes strode from the SUV, magnificent in the face of crisis. She passed the stunned onlookers with barely a glance, pausing only to look at Gwen, standing in mute shock, staring at an abandoned shoe.

Agnes smiled tightly at her, then lifted up a loudhailer. She was speaking to the crowds, she was speaking to the news crews filming from a distance, she was speaking to the helicopters that were now buzzing cautiously above the mass, and, Gwen realised, she was speaking to the creature itself.

There, on a ravaged car park off the Penarth Road, the Vam was addressed by a confident woman in a thoroughly starched dress, neatly tied bonnet and spotless gloves.

'My name is Agnes Havisham, and I claim this creature on behalf of the British Empire.'

XI

MRS GENERAL

In which Captain Harkness finds himself overruled,
and he seeks consolation from a surprising quarter

Across galaxies of suffering, the Vam had seen many
things. But even it popped out a few dozen extra eyes to
survey the woman standing calmly in front of it. She did
not seem afraid.

Curious.

Jack hadn't even made it out of the car. At the sound of
Agnes's words, he sank back into his seat with a groan.
Ianto Jones had seen Jack Harkness shot, stabbed and
shagged to death, but only now did he see the life go out
of him.

Ianto hurried round to him. Jack sat in the car seat,
eyes fixed quietly on the flickering blue dashboard. He let
out another groan and shut his eyes. Ianto stood there,
torn between staying with Jack and running over to
Agnes and Gwen.

When Jack spoke, his voice was little more than a

whisper. 'If I count to ten and open my eyes, will that woman still be here?'

'I'm afraid so,' said Ianto quietly.

'Lie to me.'

'She will most certainly be gone, yes.'

'I don't pay you enough.'

Jack opened his eyes and looked at Agnes with a despairing fury. He hoisted himself out of the car, his hand, just casually, brushing through Ianto's hair. 'Enough of this,' he said, his voice firm.

He pulled his coat around him and strode over to Agnes.

Agnes was staring defiantly up at the Vam, while also quietly acknowledging the focused searchlights of the world's media. She stared raptly into the black shimmering mass of the beast and smiled.

Gwen stood next to her, her face streaked with tears.

'Jack,' said Gwen. 'You missed some pretty fantastic people.'

'I know,' he said quietly, and turned to Agnes. 'Agnes…' he began softly.

The smile snapped off and she turned to stare at Jack, an eyebrow raised.

'Enough of this,' said Jack, his voice sounding like a grinding millstone. 'Enough bloody bonnets and la. It was all very well as a private joke, but it stopped being funny when you started World War Three.'

Agnes blinked, then grinned. 'You treasure,' she said,

sweetly. She swept a lace-wrapped arm up towards the creature. 'That, Jack, is the future. And it is beautiful.'

'This is sick,' said Gwen, loud and fierce.

If Agnes was disappointed, she didn't show it. She tilted her head, slightly. 'Yes, Mrs Cooper, it is. But it is progress. I discover that the twenty-first century is a slave to oil. It can't escape – every alternative it explores is more costly, more destructive, more futile than making energy from fossil paste. And this creature is the answer: it takes almost anything – *anything* – and converts it into the fuel you are so dependent on. Very efficiently, I might add. Wales has overnight become the most oil-rich country in the world.'

Ianto made a noise. If it had been anyone else, it would have been described as a wolf whistle, but this was Ianto.

Even Jack blinked.

'No,' Gwen stood her ground. 'I've seen what that creature does! It is vicious, it is cruel, and we've got to stop it.'

'Gwen's right,' shouted Jack. 'That creature kills. That is all it does. It devours. Look at it – you saw what it did in that toy store. How can you possibly even think of this? We have to destroy it. It's like asking Hannibal Lecter – oh you won't get that, will you… Look, it's like asking a cannibal to do your catering.'

'No.' Agnes was firm. 'No one ever said progress was pretty. Every time I wake up, I must confront a world more ugly, horrible and desperate than the one I left behind.

A world that's made terrible choices. That creature is abhorrent. But it is also useful. We must contain it, we must exploit it. It is what Torchwood was set up to do – to make the most out of alien threats. Queen Victoria would be proud.'

'And what are you proposing to do?' Gwen was bitter. 'Dig a big pit and throw people at it?'

Agnes was slightly stung. 'Not at all. A pit is a capital idea, although I suspect we'll have to find something stronger to contain it. Mr Jones has shown me your World Wide Web, and I have not squandered the opportunity. In terms of food for the creature – why, you are a nation of waste plastic, plastic that was until recently shipped out to China to be picked over by children. Until your Global Financial Meltdown, that is. Since when it has simply sat in vast, ugly piles, growing and spilling out across the country, every bit as vile as this creature. We shall simply pour all that rubbish at this excrescence, and then harvest the results. We'll make the Empire great again. Why, in two decades, with a little bit of careful husbandry, Great Britain will be the only country left with any oil. This may be a very ugly goose, Mrs Cooper, but the eggs it lays are still golden.'

Jack realised sadly that his moment of strength had passed. Oh, Gwen was furious with her, sickened by the creature, but something about Agnes's solution struck her as revenge. She was watching Agnes with the same curiosity that Ianto now was. He realised Jack was studying him sadly and glanced down.

'Agnes! Think what you're doing!' begged Jack before turning to his team. 'Can't either of you see this is nuts?'

They both looked at him, sheepishly.

'Um,' said Gwen. 'A lot of what we do is nuts, Jack. Working with you has taught me never to rule out a solution just because it's out of the ordinary. What if there is something in Agnes's discovery? God knows, this creature deserves whatever hell we can invent for it.'

Ianto kept staring down at the mud. 'I think it's worth exploring,' he said. He thought about the pictures they'd found of Chinese children picking across fields where rice had been grown for centuries. Now those fields were covered with bottles and plastic bags and sandwich cartons and juice boxes.

Agnes met Jack's gaze and smiled sweetly. 'You see, Jack?' she continued. 'If, occasionally, you look at something alien, not just as a threat, but as an opportunity, then true progress can be achieved. But I would like to thank you all for such a stimulating and refreshing exchange of views. It is most welcome. Ah!' At that, she looked across the car park to where a large, black, official-looking car had drawn in.

'That was quick,' she said, slyly. 'I suspect I am about to be reasoned with. A bit swift for the Prime Minister, but no doubt someone with impeccable credentials. The first of many.'

She turned and started for the car, a smile on her face. And then she turned, and looked at Gwen. 'I am sorry for what the creature has done, Gwen. Believe me, we shall make it pay. And,' turning slightly, 'Jack, let's resume this fascinating discussion later.'

It was early the next morning.

'Rhys! Visitor for you!' cooed Large Mandy from the outer office.

Bloody great, thought Rhys, staring miserably at the vast pile of paperwork in front of him. What he didn't get about the paperless office was how much paper there was, everywhere. Even with GPS there were still invoices, purchase orders, receipts and even the occasional tachometer to be gone through.

Gwen hadn't come home last night. Which wasn't really that unusual, given her really quite unique job, and the world ending, but still... you know. Even if she crawled in at two and slipped out before dawn, he still knew she'd been there. She'd come home. And that was, somehow, nice.

But not a sign. Not even a call. Just a text message: 'Love you, don't be afraid, call you later xXx.' That had sent the spiking horrors jumping up his spine.

Worse, he'd come in this morning to discover the Bryant account worse than ever. Stuff was still going missing from their shipments. He had scheduled different vans, different drivers, even a different depot, but always something went astray – usually fridges. Nice ones. He stared, mystified at the paperwork, and suspected a trip down to one of the discount white goods outlets off Newport Road might help.

But first, something about a visitor. So long as it wasn't Mr Bryant himself. Anything would be better than...

Oh God.

'Rhys, hi!' said Captain Jack Harkness, sitting down.

'She's dead, isn't she?' said Rhys.

Jack frowned, 'Sadly no...' And then his face cleared. 'No! Lord no! Gwen is fine, Rhys. Honestly. Fine.'

'Then why are you here?' asked Rhys stiffly. He hadn't got over the shock, truthfully. He lived in fear of something terrible – a last, brave phone call from Gwen, or finding Jack stony-faced outside his flat or... here.

Jack sensed Rhys's discomfort, and spread his hands out. 'Sorry to call on you. It's a bit... difficult.'

There was a tiny tap on the door, and Large Mandy squeezed herself in. 'Can I offer you something to drink?' she giggled excitedly. Rhys quivered. He knew that Jack was going to take some explaining. Mandy lived a life of reasonable certainties that just about fitted into a bungalow in Troed-y-rhiw. A life that didn't ordinarily include a man with movie-star good looks, a twinkling eye and a vaguely military uniform covered in dust and green slime.

'Gin would be lovely,' said Jack firmly.

Mandy giggled. 'Oh no, my love,' she said. 'We've got tea or instant. And I can probably find you a digestive.'

Jack swung round to look at her, his smile whacked up to 11. 'This instant coffee? Would it be a very cheap brand?'

Caught out, Mandy flushed slightly. 'Oh, well, more of

a discount really. Special offer. It's not branded, see, and quite powdery, but Ruth, she swears it's—'

Jack's smile peaked. 'Wonderful. I would love a cup of your unbranded instant coffee!' He winked, and turned back to Rhys, just in time for Rhys to catch what looked like a smirk of childish rebellion on Jack's face.

Mandy, thrilled beyond measure, left the office. Humming to herself.

Jack looked at Rhys.

Rhys looked at Jack.

'Hi,' said Jack.

'Hello,' said Rhys.

'So, been busy?'

'Oh, yes, thank you. Mustn't grumble. Yourself?'

'Oh, you know. Plates spinning. Balls in the air.' Jack looked evasive. For a second his attention seemed to wander, out of the window with its slatted blinds, and across the industrial estate. 'Not been watching the news, have you?'

Rhys laughed, and spread his arms out to encompass the spilling manila folders. 'Too tired last night, and straight in this morning dealing with this. Fridges going missing.'

Jack glanced at the folder and shrugged. 'Someone's trying to repair a cryogenic unit. Interesting. Tomorrow's problem.' He stared back out of the window, and then with difficulty refocused on Rhys. Rhys realised, with a slight chill, underneath the meringue that was Jack's personality, he was worried. Frightened.

'Why are you here?' asked Rhys. Direct questions often worked best with shifty drivers. And, it seemed, with Captain Jack Harkness.

'I need your help.'

'Blimey,' said Rhys. This was interesting. In the same way that bad medical results were interesting.

'I know,' and Jack smiled. 'I have an outrageous proposition for you.'

'Really?'

'Oh yes,' Jack suddenly looked like he was enjoying himself again. 'How do you fancy going behind your wife's back and saving the world?'

XII

CONTAINING THE WHOLE SCIENCE OF GOVERNMENT

In which a conference of great import is held, Mrs Cooper
prevails, and Mr Williams embarks on a hunt for the forbidden

It was early morning. Gwen came at a walking run across
the car park, bringing with her three men in indifferent
suits with important briefcases. Their drivers stood at a
safe distance. Agnes strode over, and favoured each one
with a gloved handshake as Gwen introduced them.

'We'll duck behind here.' With a gesture, Agnes
motioned them to a big brick wall. 'The fire service
are doing some decent work at keeping it at bay with
detergent, but we've also established that the creature
doesn't really eat brick. Much. Come along, gentlemen.'

Nervously, they followed her.

'Er,' began one, immediately losing any advantage.
'Miss Havisham... are we safe?'

Agnes's eyes widened with mock alarm and she
looked over at the Vam as though seeing it for the first
time, then she glanced back at her audience and smiled.
'Gentlemen, that is a relative term. But I have enough

respect for bureaucrats not to let them be eaten by an opportunity. It is not in my interests.'

'Torchwood hasn't always been so safety conscious,' muttered another.

Agnes pretended not to hear and pressed on. 'Shall I précis the situation, or did you all read my notes on the journey over?'

The third man waved his copy of the document. It had significant portions covered in highlighter pen. Agnes nodded, approvingly.

'This creature is living oil,' she told them. 'It offers the United Kingdom, nay, humanity, its greatest hope in an energy-starved future. We feed it plastic, it gives us oil. Careful control of this will make England great again.'

The third man, who had a Welsh accent, coughed slightly.

'The peoples of England, Scotland and Northern Ireland will all owe an enormous debt to our Welsh brethren, of course,' Agnes continued, smiling at all of them as though the slight slip was amusing. 'Now, the grisly truth is that this creature is not pleasant. Is it, Mrs Cooper?'

The three men's eyes wandered over to Gwen. Gwen hurriedly hung up on another irate official and smiled tightly. 'It eats everything. Including people. So far the death toll is almost fifty.'

'Can that be kept quiet?' the first man demanded.

Gwen's expression wavered slightly before she answered. 'Well, if that's decided as being absolutely necessary… But I'd argue for transparency and honesty here. Really I would. This is quite a radical solution and people should be… well, I think everyone deserves a right to know the truth. Sooner rather than later.'

'Quite,' said the second man, favouring Gwen with a patronising smile. 'It is an alien, after all. People don't expect anything else from their aliens, and they demand nothing less than to be protected by their Government. And –' here he attempted some bonhomie – 'I'm sure if it's being looked after by two such fine women, it'll be kept on a very strict diet.'

Gwen and Agnes both tilted their heads slightly at this, caught each other doing it, and turned quickly back to the creature before their grins could be seen.

'It's important,' Gwen continued, 'that people realise the true nature of this creature. It isn't a benign alien ambassador. It is petrol that hates you.'

'A chemical process with menaces,' said one of the men, and nodded. 'Thank you, ah, Mrs Cooper,' he said. 'We don't want the Animal Rights people on our backs.'

'Oh,' said Gwen, surprised. 'I'd genuinely not thought… You see, there's every evidence that this creature is a plague. It arrives on planets, and it consumes all life on them. It's here on Earth now. We can't immediately find a way to get rid of it. For the moment, we propose containing it, and harvesting energy from it through managing its size.'

'Quite simply,' said Agnes, folding her hands, 'if we don't do this, it will destroy us all.'

'Tough sell,' muttered one of the men, and another nodded.

'Like all truths, it is not easily palatable,' admitted Agnes. 'But are you familiar with the old medical practice of *mummia* – grinding up Egyptian mummies into a powder to be ingested? A practice which I now believe is deplored as both a desecration of the dead and a waste of valuable archaeological material. Yet what do you do every time you fill up your motor car? Sealed within the Earth's crust is a priceless, limited stock of ageless history – and a little more of it gets depleted every time you start your car engine. Why else is it called fossil fuel, hmm?'

'Well,' said the first man, and then petered out.

Agnes pressed on. 'In future years, the practice will seem as quaint as *mummia*. Instead, you'll be converting all of mankind's waste into food for this creature, in return for which… fuel. It is quite the most…' A pause. '… the most Green policy anyone could put forward.' She favoured everyone with a smile.

The three men's eyes drifted up to the creature, and then back to Agnes.

She nodded. 'Oh yes, it is ugly but it is the future.'

'You have to see,' ventured the second man, 'that it's a bizarre concept.'

With a cough and a shrug, Gwen caught their attention. 'The biggest producer of greenhouse gases on the planet is the cow. Scientists have been looking at harvesting their expelled methane as a viable energy source. Surely this is a little less strange than cows waddling around fields with bags to catch their farts?'

Agnes clucked with mild disapproval at the phrase.

'What's the next step?' asked the third man.

Ianto, who had arrived silently, read from a clipboard. 'Torchwood are working on some viable solutions for containment. Tests suggest that this creature has grown remarkably.'

'How remarkably?' asked the first man.

'Ah,' said Ianto, flicking over a couple of sheets. 'Probably the size of a pea yesterday.' He gestured with a neat cuff up to the wobbling mass dominating the skyline. 'And growing. From our point of view, we'd need to keep it to a manageable size.'

'The easiest thing would be to evacuate Wales,' said Agnes.

The third man spluttered with alarm.

'However,' hurried on Ianto, 'bearing in mind the old adage that oil and water do not mix, we're investigating an offshore containment facility. There are a variety of technologies that Torchwood has unique access to that could facilitate this facility.' He smiled weakly at the end of the sentence. 'If you see what I mean.'

The third man looked at him sternly. 'Somewhere like Neath?'

Ianto nodded. 'Not exactly a region of unspoiled beauty as it is, is it?'

'I have a question,' said the first man. 'Where is Jack Harkness? Isn't he normally in charge of Torchwood operations?'

Ianto and Gwen didn't even flinch as Agnes's voice rang out clearly. 'Captain Harkness is exploring other options. In case successful containment of the creature proves impossible, I believe he is preparing to kill it.'

Good luck with that, thought the Vam, amused.

Jack pulled the test tube from his pocket and placed it on the table.

'That it?' asked Rhys, mildly horrified. He poked the tube with a pencil and it rolled slightly, the black substance inside failing to move.

'Yup,' said Jack. 'A slice of the creature that could eat this planet. Oh, don't worry – once you separate a chunk of it from the whole, it stops being alive and just becomes… well, crude oil, pretty much.'

'So Cardiff is about to be eaten by a giant oil slick?'

'Yup. And we need to find a way of destroying the tar baby. It's already eaten SkyPoint, a warehouse full of toys, a lot of decent people, and an estate agent. And I think it's planning its next move – and I bet it'll be a big one.'

'OK,' said Rhys, leaning back in his chair slightly. 'And I presume you've looked into the obvious way of destroying it?'

'What?' said Jack. 'Detergents? Yeah, they're slightly effective at containing the spread of it. But…'

'No,' sighed Rhys. 'A match.'

Jack blinked.

Rhys smirked.

'Afraid not, Rhys,' sighed Jack. 'It's got some kind of molecular shielding that's annoyingly effective. As I said – carve a slice of it off, and it's no longer sentient or shielded and burns quite nicely. But as a single lump it's rather neatly fireproofed – probably the same ah, electrical processes that must contain its consciousness also form a neat barrier or dispersal mechanism. I'm not really certain.'

'Right,' said Rhys. 'And you want my help fighting something you're not quite certain about?'

'Oh yes,' said Jack. 'Agnes Havisham has convinced Gwen and Ianto that we can exploit it. She woke up two days ago and already she's trying to solve the world energy crisis. Rubbish in, diesel out. Big whoop.'

'I can see her point,' muttered Rhys, imagining running his fleet on a fuel bill of zero.

'Yeaahhhh,' Jack pulled a face. 'But this is why I've come to you for help. You're an original thinker... You know...'

'Easily intimidated by your good looks and military bearing?'

Jack nodded. 'Plus you've got a lot of trucks, and we're going to need a lot of trucks.'

Rhys rubbed his hands together, and noticed that his palms were sweating. 'What makes you sure you're right?'

'It has a name,' said Jack. 'It referred to itself, just once, as the Vam.'

'Value Added Material?' laughed Rhys.

147

'What?' said Jack.

'Oh. It's one of those geek things. Like, you know, the extras you get on DVDs and stuff. Why?'

'It's not that. I've looked it up – in all the records that Torchwood has… acquired… from alien species, there isn't a single mention of the Vam. The creature is not a new thing. Which suggests that, if it is a devourer of worlds, it is spectacularly successful. No one who has ever heard its name has survived.'

'Oh,' said Rhys.

A silence settled between the two of them.

'Or,' shrugged Jack, helping himself to the last digestive biscuit, 'maybe it is the miracle solution to Earth's environmental crisis. What do you think?'

The three men in suits got into their cars and drove away. Ianto neatly packed up the canvas chairs. Agnes turned to Gwen. 'Well, that went reasonably well, all things considered,' she said.

'Uh-huh,' said Gwen.

'Mrs Cooper, we are attempting to sell a whole new paradigm for living to three dull men who hold office. I am optimistic of success, but not one hundred per cent.'

'What else do you suggest?' asked Ianto.

Agnes pointed to the distant cameras that had been churning out increasingly baffling and abstract reports on a possible chemical spill or gas explosion on the Penarth Road. 'We take it into the public arena. We let the people decide.'

'Umm,' said Ianto. 'It's very hard to do good PR for man-eating slime.'

For an instant, it looked like Agnes was about to say something gung-ho, but then her shoulders slumped and she looked up at the giant, wobbling black creature. 'Yes,' she exhaled slowly. 'It is, isn't it? But if we don't try something, it will consume the world.'

Jack marched Rhys across to the water tower. 'I'm taking you in the flashy way,' he said.

'Your flying lift thing?' asked Rhys.

'Yup.'

'Lovely.' Rhys eyed the giant silver fountain. 'And that never fails to impress, does it?'

'Nope.'

They stood on a certain paving slab. Which clicked imperceptibly and then started to slide down into the Hub.

'Thing is, the Missus has already shown me it, mate.'

'Ah,' said Jack.

They started to sink out of view of an unconcerned Bay.

'Actually,' admitted Rhys's voice from the void, 'it's still bloody impressive. Does it just have the one speed?'

There was the tiniest of pauses. And a click.

'Wheeeeeee!'

Deep in the Torchwood Hub were many things hidden away for the good of humanity. There were cells, there

149

were vaults, and then there were storehouses. There were bunkers, there were chambers, and then there were the Schrodinger Cubes. And, finally, there was a very tightly locked door labelled *Weapons*.

'Right,' said Rhys as Jack spun a submarine-style wheel and tapped away at a keypad. 'What's that?'

'Entry coder,' sighed Jack. 'Not even Ianto has the algorithm to this. This stuff is *verboten*.'

'Enormous stash of ray guns? Can't think why,' muttered Rhys.

'Exactly,' said Jack. 'Now, Old Torchwood, they loved a death beam. There was talk of trying to win the First World War with one. Can you imagine that? Cybernetically enhanced soldiers striding through the trenches, blasting the enemy away into thin air? The death toll might not actually have gone up all that much, but it would have done wonders for the stench. And the vermin.' Jack shut his eyes while he tapped in the last few digits.

'You talk about it as though you were…'

'There?' Jack nodded. 'I'm very well preserved. Sometimes it's a bit of a curse. Handy on the dating scene, rubbish on the battlefield. Nice thing about not sleeping much is the lack of nightmares.'

He swung the door open. A rush of cold, damp air washed over them, and they stepped into a room as old fluorescent lamps blinked lazily into action. It was a large warehouse. Rack after rack of curiously shaped objects stretched before them. Some needed to be carried by ten men, and others would have fitted snugly in the palm of a baby's hand. Most of them had one thing in common – a sharply pointed business end.

'Cool,' said Rhys.

'Oh yeah,' agreed Jack. 'Every Boy Toy you could imagine is in here. And I try and ignore every single one of them on a daily basis.'

'But you're willing to make the odd exception—' Rhys reached out a hand for something small and blue on a nearby shelf that looked like a teddy bear. 'Aww…'

Jack slapped his hand away. 'Really, don't.'

Rhys chuckled. 'Rookie mistake?'

'Oh yeah. Just be glad you've still got the bones in your arm. Now, what we're looking for is alien and green.'

The two of them paused and looked around them. And looked. And looked.

The Vam lifted and surged, beginning a slow slide away from the gutted foundations of the toy shop. It was moving with deliberate slowness, generating a false impression of its abilities. It had spent the day expecting some gloriously futile military response. Instead… this. It rarely paid attention to individual members of a species but it decided that those three people down there… something about them.

It watched the fire crews run ahead of it, trying to impede its progress by spraying the road with chemicals. It allowed itself to be slowed down.

Gwen snapped her phone shut.

'Well?' asked Ianto.

'I've had better days,' said Gwen. She nodded to where Agnes stood, looking quietly at the creature. 'There's a lot of people demanding some kind of say.'

Agnes waved a hand without turning around. 'I know, I know. But I've placed the situation in the hands of the Government. And until they answer, we are deliciously unable to parley with other parties.'

'It's on the move,' muttered Ianto, watching the bulk start to slide like a cross between an avalanche and a jelly.

'Great,' said Gwen. 'I'd better try and shut off some more roads.' She snapped her phone open again.

Rhys stood uncertainly on an ancient wooden stepladder trying to hook an arm round a dusty wooden box.

'Remind me,' he sighed, feeling his tendons stretch as he brushed against the near edge of the box without falling off. 'Why's it me up here?'

'Cos I love the view,' came Jack's voice from the bottom of the stepladder.

'Cheeky. Wait till I tell the wife,' Rhys shouted back, inching the box a trifle closer. 'What would happen if I dropped this box on your head?'

'Well, there'd be a big bang, they'd have to redraw the maps of the Bay, and I'd get a large bruise.'

Rhys brought the box a little closer and, gingerly clutching it to his chest, began to wobble down the ladder. 'Got them, I think.' He skipped the last few rungs and slid to the ground next to Jack. 'There!' he beamed, handing the box over. 'Are these grenades?'

'Nope.' Jack shook his head and opened the box.

They both looked inside.

'Is that it?' asked Rhys, disappointed.

Gwen listened to the angry shouts of the Traffic Police for as long as she could. 'Look, I appreciate that,' she said. 'But there's nothing I can do to stop it from moving, so it really is over to you guys to do your best.'

There was more shouting.

'I can't say exactly what it is. No, that's "can't" as in "don't know" rather than "shan't", but believe me, it's as lethal as any chemical spill and a bit nippier. So it's best to treat it as the worst chemical spill ever. Keep everyone well back. Yes, I have seen the news and yes, that looks like it, and yes… there is a lot of it… and… thank you.'

She hung up.

'Would you like me to handle the next call?' asked Agnes pleasantly, looking round from the shuddering bulk as it shifted its inexorable, foul way onto the main Penarth Road. In the distance, Gwen could hear the wail of fresh sirens and the angry blaring of horns.

Gwen shrugged and rang Rhys. She was justifying it as 'warning him of potential major traffic disruption' rather than 'calling in for a bit of sanity'. There was no answer.

She nearly rang Large Mandy in the office to check on his whereabouts.

Agnes marched over to where Ianto was conferring

with a clutch of policemen. 'Well,' she said, 'I fancy it's time we tested those force-field barriers.'

Ianto opened up a metal case and started handing the policemen squat boxes. 'Now,' he said to them. 'Any of you home cinema fans?'

A hand shot up.

'Excellent. Dolby Surround Sound?'

The policeman nodded.

'Bugger to set up, wasn't it?'

Another nod.

'Well, this is like that. These are portable force-field generators. Stick one on top of your squad cars and reverse very slowly down the road and try and keep in line with each other. In theory we should have a barrier that keeps that creature at bay.'

'Can we see it?' asked one of the policemen.

Ianto made a face. 'Sadly no. We're not the Watchmen,' he said. 'No blue sparkles. It's invisible. But each box will emit a little ping – uh – PING! – happy sound if it's in line. You'll get two pings – PINGPING – if it's wandering slightly and then, if the field has collapsed you'll hear PEEPEEPPEEP. At that point, please get out of your car and run.'

He handed round the little boxes.

'Any questions?'

A hand shot up. Ianto ignored it. 'Right – off you go. Drive carefully. You are all that's between that monster and Ikea.'

The policemen shuffled away, and Ianto exhaled.

'Do you think it's going to work?' Agnes asked him.

Ianto shrugged. 'In theory, but I just don't... you know... There's something about that creature.'

'We will tame it,' said Agnes. 'You have to believe that.'

Ianto watched the police cars swerve around the creature and then out into the road. A distant pinging sounded. 'Well, if we fail, I'm sure the Americans will invade.'

The lift snapped into place with a gust of cold air, and Rhys found himself standing in front of the Millennium Centre, its entrance blocked by four trucks, their drivers stood smoking and muttering in front of them.

'Hi guys!' he said, and they suddenly noticed him striding towards them carrying a bulging Lidl bag.

They mumbled hello. 'What's in the bag, Rhys?' one of them chuckled.

Rhys dropped it at their feet. 'Lads,' he said. 'How do you fancy a spot of Black Ops?'

Jack bounded up as the trucks rattled off. 'Happy?' he asked.

'Double overtime, hundred quid bonus, course they're happy,' said Rhys. 'They're not going to be in any danger, are they?'

Jack reached into his pockets, peeled off a roll of banknotes and slipped them into a crumpled brown envelope which he handed to Rhys. He shrugged. 'To be frank, humanity's got a few days left at most. So I wouldn't worry too much – but they should be fine.'

'OK,' said Rhys uncertainly. 'Where were you?'

'Belt and braces – much more fun to undo both,' Jack smiled. 'I was picking up something from the medical bay. Let's get back to Mr Blobby. Now, where's my transport?'

'Ah,' said Rhys.

The Vam looked at the police cars with their force wall. It stretched out to it, gently extruding feelers, working out the size and shape and distance of it. And, all the time, it let its pace match that of the cars.

It let them think that it was contained.

Gwen put down the binoculars. 'It's going OK,' she breathed.

Agnes shook her head. 'I am not so sure.'

As each car rolled back along the road it went ping… ping… ping.

When the Vam roared out and poured over the force shield it did so in about ten seconds. It simply flowed around it, regrouping and isolating the police cars, gently crumpling the force field as it went.

Peep. Peep. Peep.

The policemen threw open the doors of their cars and ran for their lives.

**

Agnes shut her eyes and, very quietly, said, 'Damn.'

'What's the next move?' asked Gwen.

Agnes stepped out onto the road. 'Well,' she said, slowly, 'Contact Captain Jack Harkness. I am going to go and talk to that creature.'

The Vam watched Agnes approach. Her step was measured, her appearance neat. She raised her loudhailer.

'Good day,' she said. 'I should like to speak with you.'

The Vam stopped moving.

Agnes stepped closer.

The Vam quivered gently in the breeze. It appeared to be listening.

Agnes breathed deeply and got ready to speak.

A seagull settled on the Vam and vanished. Agnes watched its alarmed struggles briefly, and then raised her loudhailer, keeping her voice controlled and calm.

'I should like to speak with you,' she repeated. 'I believe it would be best.'

The Vam shivered in the wind.

'One last chance,' said Agnes. 'I wish only a good outcome for everyone. Others will come after me who are not so well intentioned.'

She lowered the loudhailer and folded her arms.

And then the Vam ate her.

XIII

APPEARANCE AND DISAPPEARANCE

In which the plans of a steel soldier are thwarted, the Vam learns of its true nature, and Mrs Cooper is betrayed by an egg

Gwen gasped.

'Not good, not good,' said Ianto.

'Jack,' said Gwen, and frantically dialled his number. 'We really, really need you.'

It was hot at the top of the crane. The cabin spun as the arm swung round erratically. Agnes lay semi-conscious on the cabin floor. The steel soldier turned at the sound of the door opening.

Battered, bleeding, but still going, Captain Jack Harkness hoisted himself into the cabin.

The steel soldier stared at him with his metal face. 'Jack!' he cried, his voice slurred. 'Enough!'

Jack steadied himself with difficulty. 'No, Sergeant. I'm not giving up till I stop you.'

Agnes dragged herself off the floor. 'Harkness is like a bad penny,' she said thickly. She managed the trace of a smile.

The steel soldier grabbed Agnes and held her between the two

of them, his gun at her temples. 'Another step, Captain, and I destroy her.'

Agnes's eyes widened, and she looked at Jack in horror.

'Have you met her?' drawled Jack.

Agnes stared.

'I mean, you know, she looks pretty enough in an older sister way, but when she opens her mouth it's all pickled eggs and Baden Powell.' He shrugged. 'Shoot away, tin man.'

The steel soldier made a noise a bit like a laugh, and its artificial voice box rattled. 'You spend so much time fighting each other. Is it any wonder it's been so easy to bring you down? Especially when you answer to this bluestocking.'

'Yeah, well,' said Jack. 'Torchwood has a history of over-promoting zealous women. We were founded by one, after all.'

'The history of Torchwood does not concern me any more.' The steel solder took a step closer to Jack. 'I merely wish to end it. Now.'

'Well,' said Jack. 'Not now, really. I mean, we've still got a couple of minutes. To talk.'

'What about?'

'Oh, I dunno. Metal limbs. World domination.'

Agnes tore her mouth free of the steel soldier's grasp. 'For God's sake, Harkness, do something!'

'And she's back in the room.' Jack shrugged. 'We won't get a word in edgeways now.'

The steel soldier grinned a tin smile and turned to look at Agnes. 'I could just kill her.'

Jack nodded. 'Probably easiest.'

***

As the site of an impending apocalypse, the toy shop car park had seen a remarkable number of things, not the least of which was a battered yellow van pulling up and, miraculously, Captain Jack Harkness climbing out of it. With as much dignity as he could manage, he walked over to Gwen and Ianto.

'Gwen! Looking commanding! Ianto! Good enough to eat! Now where's Agnes?' He rubbed his hands together as though spoiling for a fight.

Gwen laid a hand on Jack's shoulder, more for her own support than for his. 'Agnes…' she began.

'… was also good enough to eat,' completed Ianto. 'Sadly.'

'Oh,' said Jack. He looked over at the Vam. 'Good luck with digesting that!' he called.

'Jack!' cried Gwen.

'What?' Jack said, mock innocently. 'She's a tough old bird. Now, let's put the poor thing out of its misery.'

'How can you?' shouted Gwen. 'She…'

'Made a bad call.' Jack shrugged. 'Happens to us all.'

He strode off.

The steel soldier tightened his grip on the trigger, pressing a mark the size of a shilling into Agnes's temple.

'Of course,' said Agnes quietly, 'once you kill me, there will be nothing to stop Jack from killing you.'

The steel soldier laughed. 'Torchwood brought me back from the dead. But this is not a life.'

'You have value to us,' said Agnes. 'And that is important.'

'Cold, isn't she?' sighed Jack. 'Comes in handy when winning people over.'

'Clearly,' muttered the steel soldier.

'Not married, either,' added Jack. 'I think she scares men off. You should put in a bid. She could do worse.'

Agnes glared at him.

Behind them the London skyline turned gently, and the crane jerked to a shuddering halt.

'We've arrived,' said the steel soldier.

'Your plan, please?' snapped Agnes.

'Simple,' replied the steel soldier. 'There is an anomaly above London. Over the East India Docks to be precise. It is currently sealed, but I am going to use this crane to activate it. That is no ordinary wrecking ball.'

'It wouldn't be,' sighed Jack.

'Probably contains a negative static electrical charge,' snapped Agnes.

The wrecking ball, swinging like a giant hypnotic pendulum began to crackle and sparkle with red and green light. It started to jump and jiggle up and down on its chain, as though being jerked by an invisible giant.

The steel soldier looked at her and chuckled. 'Science is clearly not your strong point, but if it makes you happy then yes. That ball is opening a rift. Unimaginable power will be mine for the taking, undreamt-of forces to unleash, and London will be destroyed. That will be my revenge on Torchwood for what they did to me. What have you to say to that?'

There was the tiniest of pauses. Agnes looked at Jack.

'Oh, Sir Jasper,' she said firmly.

Jack groaned. 'No, not that, please.'

Agnes smiled and sang in a voice used to bellowing hymns, 'Oh, Sir Jasper, do not touch me!'

'What?' asked the steel soldier.

The entire crane shuddered, buffeted by a sudden wind.

'What passes in Victorian society for a smutty ditty. You subtract a word with each line,' whispered Jack confidentially, shifting his balance carefully before singing back, 'Oh, Sir Jasper, do not touch!'

'I don't understand,' shouted the steel soldier, gripping Agnes's shoulder.

Wincing with pain, she sang out, 'Oh, Sir Jasper, do-oo not!'

Jack took a step to the right, the steel soldier jerking Agnes around as a shield. 'And here's where it gets fruity.' He called back, singing, 'Oh, Sir Jasper, do!'

Agnes kicked the steel soldier in the shin, bellowing, 'Oh! Sir Jasper!'

'Oh! Sir!' gasped Jack as the steel soldier punched him.

'Ohhhhhh!' trilled Agnes, ducking.

Jack rugby-tackled the steel soldier. A gun fired.

The steel soldier staggered towards the open door of the cabin, teetering on the brink. Jack lay sprawled on the floor.

Agnes straightened up, applying herself to the controls, throwing the cabin into a spin. 'Must… move… that ball away…'

'Too late,' grunted the steel soldier, trying to steady himself in the doorway.

'Nonsense,' snapped Agnes. 'Torchwood can easily contain a semi-active causal breach fifty storeys above the Docks. This is far from Doomsday.'

The steel soldier regained his balance, aiming his gun again. 'You really think so? You mad, self-deluding co—'

Suddenly up, Jack lunged. The two of them sailed out of the cabin.

Agnes concentrated on moving the crane, watching as the wrecking ball stopped glowing and reverted to dead iron. Once she was satisfied, she turned back to the cabin door and peered down.

Jack was gripping the edge of the doorframe with one hand, his face twisted with effort.

Holding on to Jack's ankle was the steel soldier, the iron bones of his hand cutting into the flesh.

Far down below them was a London pavement.

'And what do you propose I do about this, Captain Harkness?' asked Agnes wearily.

Jack smiled with effort. 'Get me up, get this clockwork soldier off my ankle.'

The steel soldier threw another arm up, seizing Jack's thigh with vice-like strength.

Agnes shrugged. 'Bad call,' she tutted, bringing her foot firmly down on Jack's hand. 'Happens to us all.'

Ianto caught up with Jack. He was standing watching the Vam slide down the road.

'Jack,' he said.

Jack nodded but didn't turn. 'Ianto?'

'I think, I really think that…'

The Vam oozed its way over traffic cones, twisting the crash barrier like paper.

'What?' said Jack.

'You might… I mean, I know that she wasn't necessarily your favourite person, but… well, Gwen certainly…'

'And?' Jack was cold. 'Awake forty-eight hours and she thinks she can solve global warming? She's not worth your tears.'

'You are such a sulky child.' Ianto no longer bothered shouting when he was cross with Jack. 'You're hundreds of years old… People I was at school with were more emotionally mature than you, and they sniffed glue.'

Jack laughed softly. 'Pritt stick?'

'Copydex, actually, but the point is…' Ianto tried to keep his anger, but it was running out.

'You certainly had a wild time behind those bike sheds.' Jack spun round, a warm smile on his face. He clapped Ianto on the shoulder, ruffling one ear with his fist. 'Come on. I'll put on a show of contrition for Gwen, and then it's about time we saved the day.'

He walked Ianto across the car park. Ianto looked up at him. 'And how are we going to do that?'

'With the cavalry, of course, Ianto Jones.'

Agnes woke up.

'My my,' said the Vam. 'This is curious.'

'As Jonah stood inside the belly of the whale, so I, Agnes Havisham, am within the beast, bravely calling on the Almighty for deliverance,' proclaimed Agnes, standing up.

All around her was the Vam, pulsing and surging in sticky darkness.

'I do not understand your words,' said the Vam, its voice ringing in her head.

'Ah,' said Agnes. 'I see that you can make yourself understood after a fashion. When it pleases you.'

'How are you still alive?' it asked, petulantly.

Agnes tutted. 'I pocketed a force-field generator. Squeeze as hard as you like, I venture I shall be safe for another quarter of an hour at least. Which is all I need.'

'Explain more.'

'Gladly. You understand the choice we offer you?'

'Perpetual slavery in a pit or the chance to destroy you all?'

'Well…' Agnes tilted her head in disappointment. 'That's certainly one way of looking at it.'

'The only way.'

'Ye-es.' Agnes was patient. 'Only you would be of such value to us. And you would be enormously well fed and cared for.'

'The Vam will not be a pet!' the darkness roared.

'Have it your way,' she sighed. 'Only… Well, what if we could destroy you?'

'You have neither the plans nor the ability.'

'True,' said Agnes. 'But I do not work alone. My colleagues disagree with me. One of them so strongly that he's gone off by himself, so furious with me that he might just have come up with something that will polish you off. Might.'

'You play a devious game. But no one, no thing, has ever won against the Vam.'

'Ah yes – you gave us your name.'

'I like worlds I am about to consume to know my name before they are destroyed. It is good for the name of the Vam to be feared, even if only for a short time before all who have heard it are crushed.'

'Well, that's ambitious, certainly,' agreed Agnes. 'But why?'

'The Vam devours. That is all.'

'And the coffins?' Her voice hesitated. 'Were they fighting against you?'

'No…' A pause. 'They were merely in the Rift. I simply… chose one as a carrier.'

'But why?'

Around her, the neat sphere of the force field flexed inwards alarmingly and the voice roared around her before forming bitter words. 'The Vam was at a low ebb, adrift…'

'You had been defeated?'

'That information is not known. But the Vam has re-grown, will continue, will devour again.'

'Or make a new start. Last chance,' said Agnes.

'I think not.'

'Very well,' said Agnes and, crossing her legs, sat down on the floor.

'What are you doing?'

'Waiting,' said Agnes, simply, a trace of boredom in her voice. 'I suspect we shan't have long.'

Gwen sat on the remains of a brick wall, kicking her feet

and watching the Vam slither along the road.

'Cheer up, might never happen,' came Jack's voice.

Gwen sniffed, wiped her nose, and replied, 'Of all the annoying arsehole things to say—'

'I know.' His voice was soft. He flung an arm round her shoulder. She looked up and realised his other arm was wrapped round Ianto. 'What is this?' she asked. 'Group hug or rugby scrum?'

'Either is fine,' said Ianto.

Jack winked. In the distance, Gwen thought she could – just – hear sirens and the roar of engines.

'Gwen Cooper,' said Jack, squeezing her tight. 'Today is a day for you to be proud of *all* the men in your life.'

Gwen stared at him for a second. Jack could almost see the arithmetic going on behind her eyes. When she counted to three, she turned and looked again at the road. 'Rhys…' she breathed, excited and alarmed.

Jack leaned over and whispered in her ear. 'If he survives this, please don't kill him,' he said.

Rhys sat up in the first truck, the small stubby device clamped on the bonnet next to a mud-spattered teddy bear. He turned to the driver, a grim-faced man who was managing to drive while making a roll-up.

'You not going to light that, are you?' he asked.

Huw the driver chuckled deeply. 'My truck,' he said.

'Yeah,' said Rhys. 'But company law actually forbids…'

Huw raised the cigarette to his lips.

'… health and safety,' Rhys finished feebly. 'Oh, go on.'

'We're there, mate,' Huw said. Lighting up.

'I am such a softie,' Rhys sighed. He switched on the communicator Jack had given him. 'Ah, Axl Rose to Red Hot Command. Chilli Peppers are in position. We are ready to rock. Over.'

Huw snorted loudly. Rhys glared at him. 'Could you wind down that window? Slightly asthmatic.'

Huw saluted with the cigarette. 'Aye aye, sir.'

Gwen listened to her radio in disbelief. 'What did Rhys just say?'

'I picked the names,' said Jack defensively. 'Not my fault he fell for them.'

Ianto smiled. 'Well, I think we're all pleased you've got over your Abba fixation.'

'Oh, come on,' said Jack. 'What's the point of Rhys if we can't have a little fun with him?'

Gwen looked at the swollen tumour of the Vam, shuddering as it slid down towards Cardiff. Then she saw the smile on Jack's face, and she grinned too. 'I don't know what you've got planned…'

'No one ever does. That's my charm.'

'… but can I issue the order?' Her voice glittered dangerously.

Jack looked at the six trucks bearing down on the Vam from both sides of the road. 'Go on.'

Gwen reached for her radio.

***

'This is Groupie One to Axl Rose and the Chilli Peppers. Let's make some noise!'

Gwen's voice filled the cabin. Rhys gave a little whoop and flicked a switch connected to the tiny stubby little thing on the front of his truck.

And the world shuddered. The air around the Vam rippled like a hot day. And the noise! Or rather it wasn't so much a noise as… Gwen tried to focus on what was happening, but her eyes danced in her head, the fluid in her eyeballs shaking. In the watering distance she could see the road, the trucks and the Vam, but everything danced and bulged. And the noise built and built in her head, like an untuned radio echoing and echoing over and over.

'… 8… 9…' yelled Rhys. The earphones were in place but still he was trying not to cry out at the sound rattling his brain.

'10!' he shouted.

And then cut the switch.

Huw stubbed out his cigarette and grinned. 'Phew,' he said.

Ianto and Gwen ran to keep up with Jack. They were converging on the Vam which still twisted and shuddered. Jack was rattling off an explanation as he thundered across the tarmac.

'Not a lot of people know this, but forty years ago the good people of Mars tried invading. Fiiinally. Nobility factor: 10, but Resistance to Flame Throwers: 1. They had these really neat sonic cannons on their armour. Now, I figured, that thing is basically just vicious jelly. And what does jelly do best? Wobble. And we also learnt that the Vam is protected through a network of tightly woven molecules which…'

'Vibrate!' yelled Gwen.

'And, if you can make them vibrate all the more with a good whack of sound, then…'

'We can destroy it.'

Jack shook his head. 'Sadly, no. This thing is much better than that. But we can use a few blasts to keep it confused. It will fight back, but if we can make it think that this is the best we've got…'

As they pelted up to it, the side of the Vam split like a ripe apricot, revealing Agnes Havisham sitting cross-legged on the road.

Brushing invisible dirt from herself, she smiled broadly. 'Captain,' she beamed. 'I knew you could always be relied upon to betray me.'

'I'm an open book to you, Agnes,' said Jack with mock hurt. 'Hug?'

Agnes stood up. 'Not just now, thank you,' she tutted, 'My personal force field is still on.'

Jack nodded. 'Thought you'd have something like that.'

'Nonsense,' Agnes chuckled. 'You hoped I would give it indigestion.'

Jack gave a shrug.

Gwen was hugging Rhys as he climbed down from the truck.

'Not in trouble am I?' he laughed.

'Oh, bloody loads,' she assured him.

Ianto Jones stood alone in front of the beast.

'Er,' he said. 'It's not dead yet.'

'Didn't doubt that for a moment,' boomed Jack. 'Great big space blob like that? It wouldn't be giving us the whole "None-who-hear-my-name-shall-live" nonsense if it could be carried off by a sonic blast. I can name at least two people who would have tried that first off. But I figured it's had to rebuild itself, so it would be weak.'

Jack was right. The Vam was weak and reeling and surprised. It had been a long time since someone had... How long? No answer rattled back along its molecular network. It sensed a weakness and it rallied. It grouped all its strength into its external shielding and reared up. It would crush these specimens, and make an example. The Vam must show no mercy!

Rhys stood watching the shuddering mass.

Huw leaned out of the cab. 'Don't get too close, mate, will you?' he said.

Rhys looked at it. Nothing more than several tonnes of foul jelly. He had an idea. Jack had said something about a protective shield. He wondered…

'Huw, mate?' he called up to the cab. 'Don't suppose you've got a match, have you?'

Gwen yelled with fear and anger as the lit match dropped onto the quivering mass of the Vam.

Thankfully, nothing happened. The external energy net remained intact.

'Hmm,' said Jack. 'There's a reason we don't use him for intelligence operations.'

'So,' said Agnes. 'We give the creature one more chance?'

Jack looked at her in surprise. 'Someone is giving monsters an easy time these days.'

Agnes risked a rueful grin. 'We could let it eat Cardiff and then see if it wants to talk. If only we could harness it…'

Jack nodded. 'I know. But humanity's got itself into such a mess with the climate… Well, they don't deserve an easy way out of it. Especially not one that gives them all the oil they could want.'

'You'll get letters for that,' admonished Agnes gently.

'Hush,' sighed Jack. 'Let's kill El Blobbo Magnifico.'

The Vam heaved itself up over them, wobbling fiercely.

'I trust you have a plan, Harkness?' asked Agnes.

'Yup,' said Jack. He pulled a small device from his greatcoat pocket. 'Welcome to a miracle of modern medicine. You see—'

The Vam towered until it blocked out the sky and then began to pour down towards them.

'Explain later,' snapped Agnes.

Jack aimed the machine and pushed a button. 'Bleep,' he said.

'Behold the feast of the Vam!' roared the Vam happily to itself.

Ianto's worst ever birthday party had included a food fight.

Watching drunken, rowing parents throw trifle at each other in a screaming fury while he gathered his friends to him, shielding as many as possible from being hit by a stray pickled onion. He never ever wanted to see that much mess covering so many people again.

Gwen had always loved that moment in *Carry On*s when Sid James fell into slurry, before emerging, wiping slime from his face while laughing his cheap-fag laugh.

Captain Jack Harkness had stared death in the face so many times. But it had so many faces, he never got bored of it.

Agnes Havisham wished she'd brought her parasol with her.

Much to its own surprise, the Vam died.

174

It exploded in a shuddering tower of black sticky diesel that spread out in a whirling oily mist that poured up across the road, the surrounding grass banks, and covered a nearby beach. After billions of deaths across millennia, the Vam ended suddenly in a foul-smelling cloud that drifted across about three miles.

'Cowing lush,' said Rhys.

'This suit is ruined,' sighed Ianto.

After about thirty seconds it stopped raining petrol and the air cleared, leaving behind a startling stench.

Jack started yelling at once. 'Wipe it off your skin! Keep it out of your eyes!'

'Your concern is noted,' gasped Agnes, cutting a remarkable figure in oil-soaked crinolines.

Jack turned to Rhys. 'Thank you, Mr Williams. I suggest you get your people out of here.'

'Mr Williams?' Agnes's attention was roused. 'Well, how pleasant to meet you.' They shook filthy hands. 'You are terribly lucky in your choice of helpmeet,' continued Agnes. 'Although I had hoped we would meet looking less like navvies.'

'Er,' said Rhys. 'Charmed.' And then he curtsied.

Agnes turned to Gwen. 'Sweet,' she whispered.

'Rhys,' continued Jack, feeling undermined again. 'Can you get your men out of here? This is going to be the mother of all clean-up operations.'

Rhys saluted. 'Right-ho, chief. Let me know when you next need your arse saving. Come on, lads.' He attempted a heroic stride back to his truck, slipped slightly, and covered the last few paces gingerly. He waved jauntily, collected his men, and walked down towards the distant cordons.

'My husband,' sighed Gwen.

They all watched him go.

Jack stood there, a grin on his face and an expectant look.

'Very well, Harkness,' sighed Agnes. 'You are dying for us to ask you.'

Jack held up the object he'd used to destroy the Vam.

'Owen's alien surgical thingy!' gasped Gwen, turning to Agnes. 'I was pregnant once, you see—'

'Indeed?' Agnes's tone was steely.

'Oh yeah, alien succubus thing. And Owen, our doctor, used it to destroy my alien love child without invasive surgery. You just point it at a body and it… ah…'

Jack nodded happily. 'Exactly. The sonic cannons weakened the external bonding shell on that creature. I banked that it would divert energy to its external shielding. And then I just used the famously tricksie Singularity Scalpel on a dangerously wide setting to shatter its innards. It was once evil diesel from outer space – now it's just an oil slick.'

'Very good,' admitted Agnes. 'Very good.' And then she went silent, brooding.

Jack missed the signals and boomed on. 'You see, Aggie, this is how Torchwood Cardiff operates. We're rough, we're messy, but we're brilliant.'

'Hear! Hear!' Gwen and Ianto toasted him, and they all giggled.

'I understand,' said Agnes tautly. 'You see me as a foolish anachronism, don't you?'

'I'm not putting words in your mouth,' Jack smiled sweetly. 'Takes one to know one.'

'Touché,' Agnes looked pained. 'I still think… No, never mind.' She glanced at her watch. 'If you'll excuse me.' Turning her back on him, she started to walk away.

'No, don't mention it. All part of the service, ma'am!' yelled Jack after her.

'Jack!' hissed Gwen, furiously. 'Don't gloat.'

'It's not a particularly good look on you,' said Ianto quietly.

Jack coughed, embarrassed.

A fleet of helicopters roared overhead and settled behind them on the bypass.

Agnes turned and flashed a thin smile at Jack. 'No doubt that'll be the Americans, Harkness. I fear they would be too modern for poor old me. I'll leave you to deal with them.' And then, quickly, she turned her head and walked briskly away alone.

Behind them came the sound of forty pairs of army boots hitting the ground, guns being cocked and orders being barked.

'Oh dear,' said Ianto. 'Do you think they're going to shoot us?'

'Well, we are standing on a lot of oil,' sighed Jack. 'It's what they normally do.'

Gwen saw Agnes cross the road and gingerly step down the sand dunes towards the beach. 'Look,' she said. 'You deal with Uncle Sam. I'll go and make sure she's all right.'

'Fine,' groaned Jack. He and Ianto turned round slowly to see the squad running stiffly towards them across the petrol. Jack leaned in to Ianto. 'So, forty GI Joes and a lot of oil… What am I bet?'

'Ten pounds,' said Ianto.

Jack looked hurt. 'Fifty, surely. For the whole lot.'

Ianto raised an eyebrow. 'I know you too well. Twenty's as high as I'll go.' He reached for his stopwatch.

'Done,' sighed Jack, and turned back to the troops, his grin full blast. 'Fellas! Hiiiiiii…'

Gwen made her way down onto the beach. The light was fading and a cold wind was getting up, which made the smell of diesel worse. To top it all, a smoky mist was rolling over the beach, making it hard to pick her way through the dunes and across the pebbles.

'Agnes!' she called out, but there was no answer, only the dismal whistling of wind through scrubland.

She forced her way round another headland, looking in vain for a trace of Agnes. She could hear the sea breaking against the beach, rushing in and then rolling out in rocky gurgles across the pebbles. She stepped carefully across it, calling out Agnes's name again. She looked around her, but couldn't see much more than the mist. She realised that she wasn't even that sure what direction the sea or the road was in. It got colder, and Gwen suddenly felt a shiver of fear. She checked in her pocket for her mobile, and squeezed it with relief. She was utterly alone.

In the distance she thought she heard voices, but she wasn't sure – it was like the fierce whispering of ghosts through the dunes.

She walked on, balancing awkwardly on the rocks. The mist cleared ahead of her, and she saw something remarkable.

Resting on the beach was what looked like a large metal egg, about two metres high. As she got near it, the sound of the sea got louder and louder. She stared at the egg. Close up it was a bronze colour, banded by neat rows of rivets. She started to walk around it. She stopped calling out Agnes's name, and instead tried calling out a tentative 'Hello?'

She stepped closer to the egg, reaching into her pocket to phone Jack.

It was at that point that someone knocked her unconscious.

All things considered, Gwen was quite surprised to wake up on a spaceship.

XIV

A CASTLE
IN THE AIR

In which two days have passed, and there is much discussion
of the disappearance of Mrs Cooper, while Miss Havisham
arranges a most unusual funeral

Rhys:

Rhys stared glumly at the pint.

Jack reached across the pub table. 'I'm sorry,' he said, squeezing Rhys's hand. 'There's still no sign of her.'

'Burrr' muttered Rhys, vacantly. 'She'll turn up. She has to.'

'Honestly,' said Jack. 'We've combed the entire beach. We've found nothing. I mean… There was a lot of mist. Visibility was very poor and… Well, the pebbles were slippery with oil.'

Rhys looked up, his eyes saggy with exhaustion. 'What are you saying?' His voice cracked bitterly. 'She fell into the sea? Is that what you're thinking?'

'No! No,' hurried Jack. 'God no. Rhys, honestly. We're still hopeful. But it's been two days. There's just been no trace of her. It's a possibility. I just can't see it being a reality. Can you?'

'No,' growled Rhys. 'My wife is still alive.'

'I know, I know, I know,' said Jack. 'I will find her for you.'

'Two bloody days,' sighed Rhys, sipping absently at his pint. 'Not a single word.'

'Agnes is distraught,' said Jack. 'We all are. It's like Gwen vanished into thin air.'

'Is it your Rift thing?' Rhys's tone was dangerous.

Jack help up a placating hand. 'We've swept the area. Not a whisper of Rift energy. Honestly, relax. She's not going to suddenly turn up having been in an alien prison for forty years.'

'Yeah,' murmured Rhys. 'But if she had, you'd say exactly that and keep her locked up in your secret facility.'

Jack shook his head. 'I wouldn't. I couldn't, Rhys. I know how much she means to you.'

They sat there, looking out at shoppers skimming past in the rain.

Rhys's phone bleeped and he pulled it frantically out of his pocket.

'Nothing,' he cursed. 'It's the battery playing up or something. Keeps doing that. Bloody phones.'

'Bloody phones,' agreed Jack, the word sounding odd on his lips.

Agnes:
Jack strode back into the Hub. It looked oddly deserted now. Suzie, Tosh, Owen, now Gwen. The only trace of

his leadership of Torchwood was Ianto pottering around in a corner. The last remainder. He looked exhausted.

Indefatigable as ever, Agnes strode across the Hub towards him, a neat, business-as-usual smile on her tidy face. 'Captain,' she said smoothly. 'And how is Mr Williams?'

'As well as could be,' said Jack, sour in the knowledge that he hadn't told Agnes where he was going. 'I needed to make sure he was holding up. Is that acceptable?'

'Oh, of course!' Agnes assured him sweetly. 'I realise that two whole days have passed since her sudden disappearance, but we must never say die.' She swept past him to her – to *his* – office. 'And how goes the clear-up operation?'

'We've got contractors nearly finished at reopening the Penarth Road. Rhys is coordinating – you know, just in case. The problem is those beaches. That diesel is tricky stuff to shift and we've got environmental groups holding us up there while they carry out assessments.'

'Another irony!' exclaimed Agnes. 'We try to save the planet, and now we're poisoning the fish.' She turned to him in the doorway and smiled, ever so, ever so sweetly. 'We really must get a move on with that. We've saved a lot of lives, but we don't want this regrettable incident lingering in the memory. However, I have decided we should exploit this delay. Our top priority—'

'Is to get Gwen back.'

'Oh absolutely,' Agnes enthused. 'But I was thinking about those coffins. Now is a time for sober reflection.

183

I think we need to bring the coffins ashore, scan them for traces of that creature, and then begin work on giving those poor souls inside proper burials. It is our Christian Duty.'

'Bu—' began Jack.

'Well?' said Agnes. 'The eyes of the world's media have shifted somewhat away from Cardiff.'

'True,' said Ianto, materialising neatly beside them. 'Scrubbing doesn't make for good coverage. Fortunately Cardiff Bay is lacking in diesel-soaked penguins.'

'Exactly,' trilled Agnes. 'And we should capitalise on this hiatus to do something about those coffins. We can't leave them at sea reminding us of mortality. I will not have it.'

Ianto:

Ianto was making tea in his butler's pantry. He boiled the kettle, swilled the pot and then started dropping in teabags ready for the morning meeting.

'Oh no!' exclaimed Agnes from nearby. 'You've got it wrong.'

'Have I?' Ianto was, truth to tell, still uncertain about tea.

'One for me, thee, Jack and one for the pot. You've put in too many bags.'

'I put in one for Gwen,' he said.

Jack:

Jack went and stood on a roof, watching Cardiff Bay. He

was still wearing the overalls he'd used to help in the clear-up. It felt good, just once, to get his hands actually dirty, and it took his mind off everything. He sensed the end of an era. Once Agnes left, that would be it. Just him and Ianto. He was fairly certain that, with a bit of charm from him, she wouldn't use her Cowper Key, and they could continue their work. If they wanted to. And he just didn't know. The cost was getting so high.

So Captain Jack Harkness looked out at the traffic's orange shimmer across the roads and the glowing lights of the Bay, and then he looked up at the sky.

Gwen:
Gwen looked down at the surface of planet Earth turning far beneath her and poured out another cup of tea.

'How is the blend this morning, ma'am?' asked a voice.

'Oh, it's fine thanks,' said Gwen, absently. She watched Africa bend slowly over the horizon.

'Not too strong?' continued the voice. 'I am afraid that the conditions in space for tea-making are not optimal. I have tried my best, ma'am, but unfortunately there are physical restraints which one cannot defy.'

'No, one cannot,' said Gwen, stifling a yawn.

'Toast-making is similarly deplorable, as I am regrettably convinced I have already informed you.'

'Yes,' breathed Gwen, spreading some butter.

'Pleasingly, however, the marmalade and other preserves are still of excellent quality.'

'Honestly,' protested Gwen. 'These are the best in-flight meals I've ever had. You're a brilliant cook!'

'Oh, you are too kind, ma'am,' purred the voice. It was rich and plummy and completely artificial, oozing from a nearby speaker. 'Kedgeree?'

'I'm utterly stuffed,' said Gwen. 'Let's save it for lunch.'

There was a tiny electronic tut at the impropriety of suggesting kedgeree for lunch.

'Would you like me to issue you with a periodical? I have a Christmas issue of *The Strand* that I believe you haven't yet perused. It contains a highly amusing acrostic.'

'No, thank you,' said Gwen, getting out of the leather chair and crossing over to the porthole. 'I'm quite happy looking at the view for the moment. My husband will be round in a few minutes.'

Gwen tried ringing again. Still nothing, no signal.

'May I remind you, ma'am, that we are travelling too fast for your telephone to establish a stable transponder signal.'

'Yeah yeah yeah,' snapped Gwen. 'Can't we slow down?'

'Negative, ma'am.' The voice was unflappable. 'I regret that our orbit is several thousand miles an hour too fast. Even then, there are issues of distance above the mast and of connecting with your registered telephony provider.'

'I'm not going to stop trying,' vowed Gwen.

'I realise that, ma'am,' the voice continued smoothly, 'and I applaud your determination. I only regret that I am forbidden from assisting.'

'Great,' sighed Gwen. 'My husband is going to be worried frantic.'

'Indeed. I've taken the liberty of putting the kettle on. Another pot of tea will relax you and promote a tranquil nature.'

'Bloody marvellous,' said Gwen. 'Thanks to you, I'm spending most of my time in space on the loo.'

The voice was silent.

Agnes stood on the quiet shore. The sea washed up and down as the crew dragged and stacked the coffins into neat rows. The beach stank of diesel and saltwater, and the mists rolled across the coffins like a graveyard scene. Jack stood next to her, watching as Ianto ticked off coffins against a list on one of his many clipboards.

'Hard work is taking our minds off things, isn't it?' said Agnes.

She marched towards the first row of coffins, running a hand slowly across it. 'Your long journey is ended, noble soldier,' she said softly. 'Welcome to your final resting place.'

Jack stood by her. 'I've seen enough of this kind of thing,' he said. 'El Alamein, Ypres, Kandahar…'

'It's not a competition,' said Agnes, gently.

'Who were they?' Jack mused.

'We may never know,' said Ianto. 'I suppose the least we can do is honour them.'

'Yes, Mr Jones,' said Agnes. 'Is this the last of them?'

'Nearly,' said Ianto. 'There's another boatload, and then that's it. All of them ashore. And no sign of any more coming through.'

'Good,' sighed Agnes. 'Then perhaps their dreadful conflict is at an end. Maybe they won. I hope so.'

'Do you think they were fighting against that creature?' asked Ianto.

Jack shook his head. 'That thing didn't leave bodies. There wouldn't be anything to bury. These are the victims of a completely different atrocity.'

'Well,' said Agnes, 'let's honour them.'

The boat headed out to fetch the last of the coffins, the mist rolling over it.

Rhys got home. He stripped off his oil-covered uniform, dropping it into a thick black sack with a Torchwood logo on it, then turned the shower on. These days there was always enough hot water. He looked around the flat, picking up a couple of cereal-encrusted bowls and carrying them sadly to the sink. He opened the fridge and grabbed at a beer and wandered back to the bathroom. Banana Boat said they'd be having drinks at Buffalo, but he didn't fancy it. He couldn't quite face lying about where Gwen was. He couldn't quite face that she might not come back.

So he stood, watching the water run, sipping his beer.

His phone chirruped briefly, but he ignored it. He'd get a new one at the weekend. Something to do.

***

Gwen swung open the door of her room. She hadn't quite called it a cell, but that was what it was. On the other side of the door was the centre of the ship, a long metal tube of riveted bronze sheets. She pulled herself uncertainly along the walkway that was neither up nor along, feeling convinced that every echoing footstep was the sound of her foot hitting space. She craned her neck to look out at the portholes and tried to work out how big the ship was. Not too big, she thought, feeling a bit dismissive. First spaceship, so best not to be snippy. But it didn't feel like a ship for hundreds, or even ten. If anything, it felt a bit like a space caravan, which was a whole notion she was convinced her mum would approve of. She hauled her way to a bulkhead, which looked like the most solid door she'd ever seen. For the last two days the door had remained shut. It had a solid wheel that refused to turn.

'I am sorry, ma'am, but this door remains sealed to you,' came the electronic voice.

Gwen sighed, trying to twist the wheel. 'I don't care,' she said.

'I appreciate that, ma'am. I regret I am unable to assist you.'

'What about the owner?' she said. 'Will I see them?'

'I am afraid the owner is not at home and cannot see you.'

'So they're off the ship?'

'Ah, no, ma'am.' A tiny, embarrassed pause. 'The owner of the ship is not at home *to you* at this present time. If you would like, I could pass on a message for you.'

'Really?' sighed Gwen. 'Well, it's the same as last time. I would like, very much like, to go back to Earth. I would like to speak to Captain Jack Harkness and my husband. And I would like to know why I am here. And… how long you plan on keeping me here? I don't know if this means anything to you, but I work for Torchwood.'

There was a pause, and a genteel click. 'Ah, yes, ma'am. We are aware of the Torchwood Institute.'

'Oh,' said Gwen. And thought about it.

'Oh,' she said again.

The beach was eerie by tungsten torchlight. Jack and Ianto stood on the edge of the cliff, watching the men carry the last of the coffins ashore.

'I'll say one thing about your Miss Havisham,' said Ianto. 'She arranges a mean funeral.'

'That she does,' said Jack. His tone was grim.

They picked their way down the path as the boat roared off into the night. All that remained were the coffins and Agnes.

'Captain Harkness, Mr Jones, good evening,' said Agnes, striding across the beach. 'I am pleased that you are here to help the fallen find peace.'

Jack nodded. Ianto could tell Jack was remembering something.

After a moment's pause, Agnes ventured, 'And I do confidently hope that we shall not have to prepare similar ceremonies for Mrs Cooper. Rest assured of that.'

Jack looked at her sharply.

'I've not really prepared a ceremony,' said Agnes simply. 'We know so little about them. I wouldn't wish to insult them by consecrating them to a god they knew nothing of, or comfort them with a salvation alien to them. Instead, all I can offer them is the ground they lie on.'

She spread her hands.

Gwen sat in her room, worried by what it reminded her of. For one thing, it wasn't really like a spaceship. Or at least, not in the 'Houston, we have lift-off', tinfoil and goldfish-bowl sense. No spaceship she'd ever heard of had a wooden bookcase crammed full of leather volumes with a padded leather chair in front of a working gas fire. The only incongruity was the camp bed she slept in.

'Computer,' she asked. 'What is this room?'

'Your bedroom and parlour, ma'am. Is there anything you require?'

'No, thank you. I meant, what is this room normally?'

'Ah, it is more usually the study. I am afraid the guest quarters aboard this rocket are sadly limited and it was decided, after some small consideration, that you would find this more comfortable than one of the storage areas.'

'Oh, there are storage areas, are there?'

'Indeed, ma'am. Handsomely provisioned for our flight.'

'Can I see them?'

'I am afraid not. They are, regrettably, in the area of

191

the rocket that I am currently unable to conduct you around.'

'Very good,' said Gwen, thinking, *I am beginning to sound like bloody Jeeves.*

Presently, the computer served her afternoon tea. It arrived through a dumb waiter – a Wedgwood pot with matching cup and saucer and a plate full of buttered scones.

Gwen ate, thinking. Then she got up, crossed to the library and selected a volume at random. In truth, she'd found the selection a little dull. The books were very heavy, curiously cumbersome, and the print quite intensely small. They'd obviously been much read, and ranged from impenetrable works of science, pompous history (mostly about the Romans), a couple of slim volumes of Greek, far too much poetry (Robert bloody Browning), and a few works of fiction. About the only one of which she'd heard was *Jane Eyre*. She was steadily persevering with it, but her mind really wasn't on it.

She found herself in a curious state. On the one hand, she was locked up, had no one to talk to, couldn't chat to Rhys, and had only a set of Improving Works to read. On the other hand, she was in space. She couldn't get over how beautiful the Earth looked from this vantage point. It had all the magic of being in a plane above the clouds, only a lot more so. Sunrise looked amazing and sunset oddly heartbreaking. She spent hours just staring out of the window in a daydream.

By craning her head, she could make out some of

the shape of the ship she was in. Pleasingly, like Tintin's rocket, it appeared to have fins and a tapering nose. It wasn't red – the surface appeared to be a worn copper and bronze, beaten about like an antique kettle.

All in all, she wasn't bored.

She thumbed through the book again, and then flicked back to the name plate. *Ex Libris...* She struggled again to make out the handsome signature, with its dashing array of loops and curls. She was no handwriting expert, but it appeared to belong to someone jolly pleased with themselves. But fair's fair, she thought. Rocket ship. That deserves a bit of smug.

She had a theory, all right, just no evidence to back it up.

It was Ianto who detected the energy signal. An alarm went off on his PDA, causing Agnes to shoot him an annoyed glance. The three of them were standing in front of the coffins. Jack was solemn, Agnes reverential, and Ianto was, truth be told, a tiny bit nonplussed. He'd been to enough funerals of people he loved that he didn't quite see the point in standing around the last rites of some people he didn't know.

Before the alarm went off, he did catch himself wondering exactly how Agnes was proposing to bury the coffins. There wasn't much sign of a pit in evidence, and he didn't relish having to dig one himself. He suspected the usual Torchwood solution of paperwork would be called upon and he'd find himself lumbered with the job of issuing docket numbers and placing all the coffins in storage. On reflection, probably much better. There was a new industrial estate in Barry he'd noticed, and, once they'd made absolutely sure the coffins posed no further threat, he'd probably rent a nice little warehouse and seal them up there.

It wouldn't be the first time he'd done that. A land registry search for 'I. Jones' would have uncovered quite a complicated array of property in his name, ranging from a disused electronics warehouse in Newport and a Wool Museum in Cilau Aeron through to an old carpet factory in Gabalfa. There was even an abandoned manse in the Brecon Beacons, which had once, briefly, been occupied by a lesbian squatters collective, who'd ignored his letters begging them to move out for their own good. He'd not felt like visiting to find out what grisly fate had befallen them.

On the whole, though, Ianto Jones preferred hiding secrets in warehouses, in neat rows, with a disarmingly tedious phrase, such as 'Geological Survey Implements' or 'International Gazetteer of Accountancy: Research Documents'. He was amusing himself by devising a suitable alias for the coffins when his PDA started to bleep.

He looked at it in embarrassed alarm, trying to work out what it was doing. At the same time, Jack's wrist-strap computer chirruped like an underfed house cat.

They both looked at their respective screens and then at Agnes.

'Agnes,' said Jack, worried. 'Something's up.'

She didn't bother to turn around, or to disguise the annoyance in her voice. 'What kind of something, Captain Harkness?'

'We're getting an energy build-up.'

'Indeed?'

'From the coffins.'

Gwen, indecently full of seed cake, set out along the corridor again, hauling herself along by the guy ropes. The corridor was the only bit of the ship that reminded her of all that stuff about artificial gravity. Somehow (and she wasn't quite sure how it worked without her brain giving notice) the door of her parlour became the floor of the corridor, allowing her to walk up the twenty metres or so to the hatchway. She couldn't work out what was up or down, and even thinking about it made her dizzy.

As she neared the hatchway, the computer spoke. 'I am afraid—'

'Oh, shove it,' she growled, and knocked heavily on the door.

'— the master is unable to—'

'Hello!' she shouted.

'— at this present—'

'Hello!'

'— and that, if you'd care to—'

'Oi!'

'— I shall make best endeavours—'

'Open up!'

195

'— pass on at the earliest—'

'Open! The! Bloody! Door!'

Gwen had tried this a couple of times before, with the firm sense that she was being icily ignored. But it was either do this, or slump back to the parlour for sardines on toast. Whoever else was on board, they were probably the size of a house by now.

Gwen continued banging and yelling and the computer continued to protest politely.

'I know who you are!' she bawled.

There was a click and a creak.

Gwen leapt back, and grabbed a handrail before she suffered the ironic fate of being the first human in orbit to fall twenty metres to her death.

With a steady, slow grinding of metal, the door groaned open and a figure was revealed.

Jack ran forward, waving his wrist-strap. 'Correction. There's an enormous energy build-up from these coffins!'

Agnes stood her ground. 'Hadn't you better keep back, then? What kind?'

'I don't know,' yelled Jack with frustration.

Ianto joined them, cross-checking the information from his PDA with Jack's computer.

'Not good, not good,' shouted Jack.

Agnes arched an eyebrow. 'Bang?' she said.

'Not exactly,' groaned Jack. 'But it's … See…!'

The coffins began to glow.

'Glowing coffins. Never going to be good.'

Agnes placed her hands on her hips.

'I think,' said Ianto, with the care and calm of a bomb disposal expert choosing between the red and the green wire, 'I think we've been operating under false principles. What if these aren't coffins at all?'

'Then what do you suggest?' asked Agnes.

'Er,' said Ianto, weakly. 'I was thinking pods. Survival pods.'

The man on the other side of the door wore a smoking jacket and a worried expression. He was a slender man of late middle age with quite comical sideburns, remarkably elaborate spectacles and a stiffly pressed white shirt.

'Oh, hello,' he said with an air of forced jocularity. 'Were you knocking?' It was an amazingly feeble lie. 'I am afraid I'm most extraordinarily busy just at the moment. How'd'y'do?'

'Right,' said Gwen, tired of this already. 'And you are?'

'Ah,' said the man, clearly embarrassed. He stretched out a hand. 'George Herbert Sanderson.'

Gwen nodded. 'Agnes's fiancé?'

The first coffin clicked open, spilling out a harsh blue light. An instant later, a hundred echoing clicks sounded across the beach, and the night was lit up an entirely wrong shade of blue. The figures that sat up, stood up and stepped out were initially silhouetted by the glare, but Jack could see that they were barely humanoid.

They looked like toadstools, or the kind of unpleasant stick dogs find for you on walks – all knobbles and whorls and glandular protuberances, like nightmare trees. They were about two metres tall, a clicking, whirling bulk of bark and moss and twitching branches without any obvious faces.

They weren't wearing uniforms, or clothing of any kind. Normally Jack liked nothing more than a naked alien, but these were the wrong kind of naked alien. Whether it was the harsh lighting, the sticky ugliness, the horrid way they slithered across the sand, or just the enormous guns they were holding, there was something about them that was threatening.

Jack pulled his own revolver and aimed it. 'Hi there!' He began, 'I'm from Tor—'

The first alien spoke, hardly aware of him, its horrible voice filling the beach with a noise like walls tumbling in a flood. 'We are xXltttxtolxtol. We have arrived.'

Agnes Harkness strode forward, arm outstretched. 'Greetings,' she said. 'Agnes Havisham. I have heard so much about you. Welcome to your new home.'

'What?' hissed Jack.

Ianto leaned close to him. 'This is an invasion. And she's organised it.'

Jack groaned.

XV

CONSPIRATORS
AND OTHERS

*In which Miss Havisham has a meeting with remarkable trees,
and Little Dorrit's secret is finally revealed*

'Shall we take tea?' ventured George Herbert Sanderson
nervously.

'Are you kidding? I'm so full of the stuff I'm sloshing.
What the hell is going on here?'

George Herbert looked as though he had never, ever
been spoken to like this by a woman.

'Come now. Perhaps a little refreshment, my dear?'
he pressed on, good manners prevailing over a face that
was thoroughly taken aback. He called up to the ceiling.
'Bramwell, a pot of tea in the Observatory, if you wouldn't
mind.'

'Of course, sir,' oozed the computer.

George Herbert rubbed his hands together. 'Splendid.
Come along.'

He steered a fuming Gwen over the threshold and into
a room which offered an even more jaw-dropping view
of the Earth. As they climbed up a spiral iron staircase

to a table laden with paper charts, Gwen noticed a tea trolley sidling unobtrusively into view. 'Sit down! Sit down!' George Herbert ordered, making a small attempt at tidying up the charts, but failing dismally. He sighed and sat down, absently drumming his fingers on the desk.

Gwen mastered her fury and went with her biggest smile. 'You are who I think you are, aren't you?' she said.

'What?' George Herbert seemed to have his mind elsewhere, and splashed tea everywhere as he poured. 'Oh, right, yes, Miss Havisham and I are betrothed, indeed. Have been for over one hundred years. Goodness, sounds funny when you put it like that. I am the luckiest man alive. Battenberg?'

Gwen waved away the plate, kept her smile in place, and gave George Herbert a piercing look. 'Aren't you supposed to be at the other end of the universe?'

'Nonsense! What a preposterous notion! Why, the universe is so appallingly big, whereas I was merely visiting a spot a few solar systems away. Practically next door.'

'But it still took you a hundred years to get there.'

'More or less, ah yes.' George Herbert looked a little uncomfortable.

'And yet not so long to get back.'

'Not so long, no. Bramwell was able to piggyback us through your Rift, weren't you?'

'Indeed sir.'

'Splendid fellow. Talented cook, excellent navigator,

but,' he leaned forward confidentially, 'sadly predictable at draughts.'

'Right,' Gwen pressed on, eagerly. 'This is brilliant news, isn't it? Does Agnes know you're back?'

'Ah…' said George Herbert hesitantly. 'Yes. Yes she does.'

'She does?' exclaimed Gwen. 'But she must be overjoyed, I mean, you're back! Early! You know… How long has she known?'

George Herbert whistled a broken bit of Gilbert and Sullivan. 'I am afraid she's known for quite some time. You see, ah, I'm sure she won't mind me mentioning this, but I have been back for several days.'

'But,' said Gwen, 'when she told me about you, she said you were a long way away and… Days?'

'Days,' nodded George Herbert apologetically.

'But why hasn't she…? I mean…'

'I am sorry,' repeated George Herbert sadly. 'This must be quite a shock for you.'

'Well, yes, but not as much as it must be for her. I mean, surely she's overjoyed. You both must be.'

George Herbert looked anything but overjoyed. His face drooped like a donkey's. 'Things are, I rather regret, complicated.'

Gwen laughed. 'I'm sure she's not met someone else! She thinks the world of you.'

George Herbert winced at the phrase. 'I'm saddened to say that she is responsible for your current predicament.'

'Yeah,' huffed Gwen. 'I'd gathered that. Somehow. I mean, I guessed it would be something like that. I'm not stupid. I figured it was because you wanted to surprise her, but, hang on, that doesn't fit now, does it?'

George Herbert shook his head. 'I am so dreadfully sorry. She ordered you brought here.'

'What?' gasped Gwen.

'What the hell is going on?' shouted Jack Harkness.

A hundred guns immediately pointed in his direction.

'Wait!' yelled Agnes, a gloved hand raised. 'Don't kill him. Well, I mean to say, you can't kill him. Just don't shoot. Thank you.'

Ignoring the mildly confused xXltttxtolxtol troops, Jack bore down on Agnes, his gun waving like an exclamation mark. 'You organised all this? The coffins? The Vam?'

The xXltttxtolxtol commander looked at Agnes enquiringly and then back at Jack. The way his gun moved said clearly, 'Surely you would like me to kill him?'

Agnes looked Jack directly in the eyes and inclined her head slightly. 'I am responsible for rescuing the xXltttxtolxtol, yes. I am shocked and really must protest at the accusation that I had anything to do with the Vam. That excrescence simply hitched a ride in the Rift.'

'But what,' asked Ianto reasonably, 'are these xXlttxt… creatures doing here?'

'It's xXltttxtolxtol, dear, and it's quite simple.'

'They're invading,' growled Jack.

Agnes laughed dismissively. 'Nonsense. That's not it at all. Isn't that right, er…?'

'My name is zZxgbtl of the xXltttxtolxtol.'

'Of course, it would be,' trilled Agnes. 'And this isn't an invasion. The very idea!'

'You see,' said George Herbert, 'it took me many years to reach the planet that the drive came from that this ship is built around. Of course, time passes inside this craft at a different rate. Agnes told me the other week that it's since been discovered and explained by a clever Jew scientist, but back then we just had to make a few educated guesses. Honestly, ninety per cent of this craft is food. Bramwell is terrified of it all going to waste, you know. Biccie?'

Gwen waved the plate away.

'So,' the scientist continued, 'I sailed off in my rocket ship, you know, keen to take the Empire out into the universe. Bit of enlightened self-interest, don't you know. Set up a trading partnership, that kind of thing. I mean, the message that we found with the drive unit was in effect that we'd learn something to our mutual advantage by visiting, so it seemed rude to ignore the invite.'

'Eh?' said Gwen.

'Well, the drive unit was part of a probe that crashed. The drive itself survived rather well, along with a full set of formulae that were reasonably easy to decipher. It was effectively a set of coordinates, together with instructions for building a ship around the drive unit. And that's an invitation, clear as day. Well, old Ralston Baines argued that it was more of a "if this probe should dare to roam, box its ears and send it home" kind of ballyhoo, but I overruled him, and got the grand wave from the old Regina to set sail for Planet X.'

Gwen blinked.

'That's what we're calling it, you see. Good name, eh? So, off I set. And when I arrived, you know, I met the natives and they were friendly blighters. Odd-looking fellows but jolly eager to learn English and all about the Earth. You see, the xXltttxtolxtol—'

'Oh' said Gwen, realising that, despite what Jack had told her, Welsh was not the hardest language in the galaxy.

'Yes, ah, yes, well, turns out they were in a bit of a pickle. Hence sending out all the probe things. Their planet is dying – only a few thousand years left in the old gal. So they were looking for likely other worlds to live on apart from doomed Planet X. The idea being that either a probe would find somewhere, or an obliging species with a spare bunk would get the message and pitch up with a set of keys.'

Gwen wondered at this. How much of this did Agnes know? How long had this been planned?

'So when I turned up, all pith helmet and Rule Britannia, they knew they were onto a good thing if they played their cards right. And I chatted about this to Aggie, and she happened to mention the dear old Cardiff Rift, which, with a few equations, the top xXltttxtolxtol boffins were able to turn into a neat little space warp, enabling me to set off with a few chums and get here early. Brilliant plan.' And here his face fell. 'Only…'

'They've got guns,' said Jack.

Agnes wasn't fazed. 'Of course they've got guns, Captain. The xXltttxtolxtol have only just met us and they're not sure of their welcome. Especially not with you waving your firearm about like a nursery rattle.'

'Those are very big guns,' said Jack.

'Agreed,' said Ianto.

'Then our welcome must be even bigger!' beamed Agnes. 'Dear zZxgbtl! How was your journey? You must be tired. You'll want a rest and a chance to get your bearings before I show you to your Guatemala.'

'I beg your pardon?' said Jack while zZxgbtl swayed in the breeze.

'Guatemala! It's a chunk of the Earth that I identified as most compatible with the xXltttxtolxtol's own environment, whilst not being terribly important. There's really not that many of them, and they'll fit in jolly well.'

'What… about…' Jack spoke slowly, 'the… people… of… Guatemala?'

Agnes shrugged. 'They'll have to budge up and put up. But it'll be of enormous advantage to us. And, as I said, it's not exactly a country that's really contributing at the moment. This is their chance to do their bit.'

'I'm sure they'll be thrilled,' whispered Ianto.

'Oh absolutely.' Agnes had heard him. 'Imagine what they have to offer. The xXltttxtolxtol are renowned poets, skilled gardeners, and wonderful scientists.'

'With very large guns,' repeated Jack.

Agnes finally snapped. 'This is rot and will stop at once. Aliens should be dealt with intelligently and creatively, not as some kind of utility menace. It's childish.'

'First you hugged the killer blob, now this,' Jack was bitter. 'I actually preferred you in the old days.'

As Agnes and Jack stood there bickering on the beach, the xXltttxtolxtol had shuffled to form a rough, interested circle around them. And now zZxgbtl spoke.

'If I might intrude upon the debate,' it said. 'The stupid male is actually right.'

Agnes's face fell. 'Oh,' she said.

'You see,' sighed George Herbert, 'I tried to warn her. Underneath that armour plating, Agnes has actually got such a sweet, trusting nature. We were both totally taken in, I fear.'

Gwen realised she was listening to the space equivalent of an email from a friendly Nigerian businessman requesting the temporary transfer of your bank details for an offer of mutual advantage. She smiled sympathetically.

'Sadly, by the time I realised that the xXltttxtolxtol were something of a threat, the coffins had already turned up and I was already here. Things had moved jolly quickly. It was all rather too advanced. I took the shuttle down to warn her that there was something fishy about them, but you turned up.'

'What?' said Gwen. 'This is my fault?'

'Well, yes, my dear. Agnes was so worried she'd miss the rendezvous with the shuttle that she wasn't as careful as she normally was. I was about to tell her everything when you turned up, and she knocked you out and ordered me to bring you up here out of the way.'

'I have a husband,' said Gwen. 'I've been gone days. Do you know how worried he'll be?'

George Herbert winced. 'I can only imagine and sympathise, but we couldn't leave you down there, and we just couldn't bear to kill you.' He leaned forward. 'Agnes really rather adores you, you know. As I said, soft as a kitten.' And he chortled fondly, spearing a crumpet on a toasting fork.

Gwen boggled at him. 'So while everyone I love is hopefully going nuts with worry and the Earth is being invaded, I'm stuck up here watching you toast crumpets?'

George looked up from the fire he was holding the crumpet over. 'Ahhh, yes. Succinctly put. But I can't see what else to do. Agnes is down there, on the ground. I'm hoping she'll sort out something clever. She's honestly magnificent in a crisis.'

'She had bloody better be,' growled Gwen.

zZxgbtl of the xXltttxtolxtol advanced slowly forward with a menacing hop, tendrils trailing through the sticky diesel remnants of Vam scattered across the beach.

Creaking branches whipped up into the air, caressing

Agnes's face. She didn't flinch, but stared straight at it.

'We are the bridgehead,' it said. 'Now we are here we shall send the signal of safe arrival back to our planet and then stabilise the Rift, allowing the proper invasion to begin. You may watch before you suffer the symbolic death of traitors. Bind them!'

Jack raised his gun, but a branch lashed out and snatched it from him.

'Great,' said Jack.

The strange, sharp, alien trees pressed in around them, rustling and twitching and occasionally prodding them with nightmarish thorny vines.

And then branches and creepers lashed out, wrapping round them and dragging each of them up onto the back of a xXltttxtolxtol, sap spreading and sticking over their clothes. Ianto whimpered as gelatinous trails seeped into the fabric of his suit. Despite himself, Jack grinned. He suspected Ianto was more worried about the dry-cleaning bill than death.

Jack fought against the bonds, but the more he struggled, the tighter the branches wrapped themselves around him. Soon his torso was completely secured.

He looked across at Agnes. She stood like a statue, trussed up ready for careful shipping. He couldn't decide if it was stoicism or defeat.

Once the binding was finished, the other xXltttxtolxtol shuffled away, leaving them planted on the beach like three witches ready for a burning.

zZxgbtl of the xXltttxtolxtol surveyed them, its

booming whisper of a voice scraping across the bay. 'You shall remain like this and you shall watch us destroy the world you have given to us. And then you shall beg to suffer the death of traitors.' And, for the first time in Jack Harkness's long life, he heard a tree laugh. And then it dragged itself away.

For a moment the three were silent, half-standing, half-crouching together, bound to their immobile wooden guardians.

And then Agnes spoke.

'Oh dear. I had planned this so very carefully,' she said quietly. She was looking sadly out to sea. 'Honestly. I advised them on the construction of the coffins so that Torchwood would be unable to analyse them. I told them all about the Rift, I even set the alarms to be triggered by their arrival. My one worry was that Torchwood One would work out what was going on, but thankfully they're gone – which only left you, and pulling the wool over your eyes was always child's play.'

Jack looked sharply at Agnes. 'You never cease to betray me.'

Agnes flashed a slightly queasy grin. 'It's always been so easy to fool you, I just can't help myself. And I was so pleased that I never considered I was being taken advantage of.' She kicked angrily at the sand with a loose foot.

Jack leaned close to her.

Agnes continued to stare at the beach. 'Don't try to be consoling,' she muttered. 'If you do, I shall scream.'

Jack placed a free hand awkwardly around her shoulder. 'You are full of surprises, Agnes Havisham. In all the years I knew you, I never ever dreamed you could be deceived.'

Agnes looked at him, startled. 'Really?'

'Nope.' Jack pulled a face. 'You always seemed ruthlessly efficient.'

Agnes sniffed bravely. 'It was all an act, I assure you.'

'It was a very good act.'

'Thank you.' Agnes folded her hands as best as she could. 'Well, it'll soon be dawn,' she said simply.

Ianto tried to shrug, but his bonds wouldn't let him. 'We're tied to trees. We're surrounded. If we try and summon help, these things will kill us. They're about to invade the Earth and there's no way of stopping them. What are we going to do?' he asked.

Jack and Agnes looked at each other and then back at Ianto. Agnes managed a brave smile.

'We are open to suggestions, Mr Jones. But I fully intend to enjoy the view.'

With only mild difficulty she reached into her muffler, and drew out *Little Dorrit*.

'Not that book!' Jack groaned. 'Everywhere you go, that damned book comes too.'

Agnes opened it up and smoothed out the first page, reading the bookplate there fondly. 'It is a familiar and valued thing,' she said. 'And pray tell if you can think of a better way to spend our last hours.' She turned over a page.

'But surely by now, you'd have finished the damned thing.'

'Ah,' said Agnes, with a little smile. 'I'm afraid that's more of a challenge than you'd think.'

She flicked to the back of the book, reached into the last hundred pages and drew out a small flask. 'Tot of rum?' she said.

And so Torchwood stood on a beach, tied to trees, watching the sun rise on the last day of Earth, passing a flask of rum between each other.

XVI

THE STORMING OF THE CASTLE IN THE AIR

In which Mr Jones's intoxication is sadly regretted in the sober light of day

Gwen yawned and looked out at planet Earth.

'The sun'll soon rise over Wales,' said George Herbert, 'and then I get to find out if I'm wrong about the xXltttxtolxtol. I sincerely hope they're just the misgivings of a natural worrier.' He looked out of the window glumly. 'Do you think she *has* met someone else?'

Gwen smiled. 'No,' she said.

'Ah well, that's good.'

'Look,' she said carefully. 'Surely there's something we can do. Maybe you can fix my phone? I'd like to speak to my husband.'

She passed it to him, and George Herbert looked at it, curiously, before addressing the computer. 'Is there anything you can do with this, Bramwell?' he asked. 'It's a portable telephonic device.'

There was a drawn-out sigh of electrical consideration. 'There are a considerable number of communications satellites sharing our orbit. It is possible, sir, that I could perhaps run a signal through one of them to link with Mrs Cooper's network. Would you enjoy another pot of tea while I try to establish a link?'

'No, thank you,' said George Herbert quickly. He crossed over to a writing desk, and pulled some wires out, cradling Gwen's phone in a mesh. 'Perhaps,' he said, 'that will help.'

Gwen stood up, and stared down at the Earth. 'Good morning, world,' she said. 'It looks so quiet.'

The xXltttxtolxtol had arranged some of the coffins into a complicated archway, churning the beach up into a gritty mixture of sand and Vam.

'You know what,' said a slightly tipsy Agnes, sagging a little in her bonds, 'I bet that's a portal.'

'Classic portal,' murmured a sleepy Ianto. His head drooped forward, resting on her shoulder. The rest of his bodyweight was carried by the tree he was bound to. Agnes gently nudged him away and he began to snore quietly.

Jack winked at her, a lazy smile on his face.

'So,' he said, 'Torchwood are powerless, one of our agents is missing, and the Rift is about to be hijacked to allow a wholesale invasion of the Earth. How would you say the assessment is going?'

Agnes chuckled darkly, 'Not so well, not so well.' She threw the empty flask out to sea. 'But you can't win everything.'

'No,' sighed Jack. 'You can't.' He belched, contentedly, and tried to reach an itch on his back.

'On the other hand,' said Agnes, pointing up at a fast-moving star in the sky, 'that, up there,' and she giggled conspiratorially, 'is a rocket ship.'

'Is it?' laughed Jack.

'Oh yes,' she said solemnly. 'And on it is George Herbert Sanderson.'

'Never!' Jack rubbed his hands together. 'So he came back to you in the end! Pleased for you. I've always found long-distance relationships a little tricky myself.'

'Well…' Agnes considered carefully. 'He has put on a little weight. His computer overfeeds him dreadfully.'

'Ah yes,' said Jack portentously. 'But that makes it harder for them to run away.'

'And,' Agnes held up a finger with a sssh, 'I've a surprise for you – up on the ship is your Mrs Cooper.'

'Gwen!' Jack was delighted. 'You hid her away, did you? You naughty thing.'

Agnes tapped the side of her nose. 'That girl is too good for you, Jack. Stick to tea boys.'

Jack watched Ianto fondly as he dribbled slightly in his sleep. 'I intend to.'

zZxgbtl of the xXltttxtolxtol dragged himself past, then stopped, waving his big gun.

'Soon, humans, soon our portal will be established and, after your ultimate despair, you will suffer the death fit for the betrayers of your own species. You will remain strapped to these xXltttxtolxtol, who will wear you till you die.'

'Ah, nailed to a tree,' smirked Jack. 'I love a symbolic death.'

'It is a very painful way to go,' said the xXltttxtolxtol.

'Ohhh, I'm sure, but it won't work, you know,' giggled Agnes.

'What?'

'I've been trying to kill him for years. Dropped him off buildings, shot him… Nothing worked.'

'Don't forget the bomb,' put in Jack.

'Lordie! How could I forget the bomb!' hooted Agnes. 'Ears were ringing for days.'

The xXltttxtolxtol hopped closer. 'Are you…' it asked, leaning as much as a space tree could. 'Are you intoxicated?'

Jack and Agnes laughed.

'Absolutely smashed.'

Ianto stirred in his sleep, snored loudly, and opened an eye. 'Missed anything?' he asked blearily.

'Nope,' said Jack, managing to ruffle his hair. 'Civilisation is still as we know it.'

The xXltttxtolxtol considered them, carefully. 'Now that the portal is established, we no longer need your relay ship,' it said.

Agnes straightened up. 'What do you mean?' she demanded, suddenly sober.

'Your sapling is surplus to requirements,' it said cruelly. It laughed, the laughter like a clattering of branches.

And then it raised its big gun, and pointed it at the sky. And fired.

A few seconds later, the star in the sky flared brightly and went out.

Agnes screamed, and Jack grasped her hand.

The xXltttxtolxtol turned back to them. 'Now, I think, you take me seriously.'

Gwen tried dialling the phone, but still nothing. She looked at it with frustration.

'My apologies, ma'am,' said Bramwell, 'but this is proving a complicated mechanism.'

George Herbert looked at Gwen's phone. 'It is a marvellous thing. Why, in my day, even the Torchwood Institute only had a single telephone. To think that you carry this around with you in a pocket. The uses must be endless.'

Gwen shrugged. 'Mostly I just tell my husband I'm working late.'

'Excuse me,' coughed Bramwell. 'Incoming.'

'Are you getting a message, old chap?'

'No sir,' stated Bramwell. 'I regret that there is incoming ordnance. It will impact the craft in—'

Gwen saw something hurtling towards them from the Earth and then a blinding, blinding light and the tearing of metal.

Agnes, Jack and Ianto stood on the beach, slumped in their bonds. They were very quiet and cold. zZxgbtl of the xXltttxtolxtol towered over them, heedless of the tide coming in and washing around his feet. If a tree could be said to gloat, he was gloating.

'Now we will open the portal and destroy your world.'

XVII

THE CHIEF BUTLER RESIGNS THE SEALS OF OFFICE

In which calling occupants of interplanetary craft becomes necessary

Gwen woke up to find she was lying on top of the Earth. It was spinning. Somehow, the rocket ship had listed alarmingly, and she was sprawled face down on the Observatory window, watching the planet rush up. She could hear the drilling of alarm bells and the crackling of flames.

Trying not to pass out from sheer vertigo, she rolled over, and hauled herself to where George Herbert lay, folded over a chair bolted to the floor. Which was now the wall.

All around her the craft shook alarmingly. We are falling, she thought. We are falling out of the sky. She wondered when it would be OK to panic. And told herself, no. Not yet.

George Herbert looked at her. There was a cut down one cheek. He used a word that Gwen thought had only been invented in the 1980s.

'They fired on us!' he cried. 'We are in a lot of trouble.'

'I'd gathered that,' said Gwen.

'There's no need to shout,' said George Herbert.

Gwen realised she had shouted. *OK*, she thought. *I have started panicking.*

'Bramwell!' snapped George Herbert. 'How are you?'

'I am fine, thank you for asking, sir. I regret to inform you, however, that our engines have been destroyed and we will impact with the planet's surface in under five minutes.'

'Fine?' Gwen mouthed at George Herbert.

He shrugged. 'Any good news?'

'Ah yes.' The machine sounded as though it was manfully ignoring pain. 'Now that we are considerably closer to the planet's surface, I have obtained a signal on Mrs Cooper's telephone. Reception is, you will be pleased to hear, getting better every second.'

Gwen had already snatched the phone out of its cradle and was dialling.

With a little effort and a hefty scratch to the wrist, Jack pulled the ringing phone from his pocket. The xXltttxtolxtol he was strapped to twitched menacingly.

'Prayer stick,' said Jack, quickly. 'I'm communing with the dead.'

Mollified, the xXltttxtolxtol grunted.

'Gwen! Great to hear your voice,' Jack hissed, delighted. 'Where are you?'

'In a spaceship crashing into the Earth,' she said.

220

'Help!'

'Ah, thought that might be the ca-case,' Jack slurred slightly. 'How's space?'

'Are you drunk?' bellowed Gwen incredulously.

Over the phone, Jack heard an explosion. He frowned. 'Tiny bit tipsy,' he admitted. 'We're on a beach in Penarth that's about to be overrun by an alien invasion force. We're tied to trees and they're pointing guns at us. Very big guns.'

'Great,' came the reply. 'Well, if you're lucky, I'll land right on top of you.'

'It's shaping up to be that kind of day,' said Jack ruefully.

Agnes snatched the phone off of him. 'Mrs Cooper,' she snapped. 'Is George Herbert with you?'

'Yes – and he's fine. Although how much longer we'll be able to… sorry? What was that? Look – I'll call you back.'

Further down the beach, the portal had started to glow ominously.

Another explosion sent the rocket ship spinning.

Gwen screamed as she felt them plunge into a dive. George Herbert reached out a hand, yelling something at her over the thundering sound of tearing metal. Gwen listened to him very carefully, and then made another phone call.

***

221

'Gwen!' The relief was clear in Rhys's voice. 'Where are you? Where have you been? Why haven't you phoned? Do you know how worried I've been?'

'I'm in space!' came the slightly thrilled, slightly panicky voice. 'Where are you?'

'Seriously? I mean, really?'

'Oh yes. Proper rocket ship.'

'I'm dead jealous.'

'Oh, I know you are. That's why I love you. Now, listen – are you near the Penarth Road?'

'Well, a bit. In a van, helping clear up after that monster thing of yours. I tell you, filthy it is, my clothes are soaked in diesel. I swear I've broken the washing machine. Oh, Gwen, it's just amazing to hear you—'

'Yes, right, yes. Just… Look, can you do something for me?'

Gwen passed out briefly. She could feel herself being shaken to pieces. The only time she'd felt acceleration like this was when she'd got lifts to work from Angela Partington, who drove her Mini at 120 on the motorway.

Books toppled from the shelves of the Observatory, flame rising from some of them as they tumbled. All around her the ship was creaking dangerously. Loosened cables swung in the air, and smoke poured through ugly cracks in the bulkhead.

She rang Jack again. 'Listen,' she said. 'No… not so good. But look, keep the line open, whatever you do.

Help is on the way. Just keep the line open.'

'What are you doing with your prayer stick?' demanded zZxgbtl of the xXltttxtolxtol, snatching it from Jack. 'This looks, in fact, like technology. Is it a signalling device?'

Jack shrugged. 'Electronic Prayer Wheel. I'm waiting for an answer from the heavens. I'm very devout. Why, Ianto and I are always on our knees—'

'Enough music-hall vulgarity,' snapped Agnes. 'Just take his little thing off him, if you must, zZxgbtl. What difference can it make?'

'Exactly,' sneered the tree. 'Any reinforcements will be eliminated. The Earth will be crushed like a dry twig.'

'Absolutely,' said Agnes. 'Considering this is your first invasion, you're doing very well indeed.'

zZxgbtl threw Jack's phone into the sand.

Gwen stared at the phone. 'He's gone! I can't hear his voice.'

George clasped it to his ear. 'I can just hear the sea,' he said, and smiled. 'Just like a shell!'

Gwen grabbed the phone and looked at the display. It said the line was still open. She hoped it was true.

George gently took the phone back from her. 'There's no time, I'm afraid, my dear. And Bramwell needs all the help he can get.' He slapped the phone into the heart of a lash-up of wires and valves. 'How are you doing, Bramwell?'

'I regret to say, sir, that I am now feeling somewhat

indisposed. However, my navigation systems are fixed on the homing signal. I am sadly unable to impede our progress.'

'That's fine, Bramwell. You've done very well indeed. And I will miss your company.'

'It has been a pleasure serving you, sir.'

'Farewell, my friend.'

George Herbert took Gwen's hand and led her from the shattered Observatory.

Their progress through the rest of the ship was erratic, hampered by having to climb the wrong way up a ladder which was hanging out of a wall that was shaking itself to pieces.

Beneath them, the Earth and the sun whirled around the portholes as the ship spun and spun. The entire rocket was rattling, the windows clouding up with a red glow as they tumbled into the atmosphere.

Gwen had never dreamt that metal could be so loud. The air howled with the noise, and she became aware that she was surrounded by shaking, melting sheets of steel, held together with little more than rivets. She might as well have been in space in a tin bath.

The ladder they were clinging to jumped, bowing out of the wall, but they held on. Gwen could feel the rungs getting hotter under her hands, and she wondered how long she could hold on for before the burning made her let go. It was insane. Her first ever driving lesson and she'd reversed Dad's car into a dry-stone wall. First time in a spaceship and she was crashing into the planet.

A piece of burning debris flew past them, and Gwen screamed. George joined in, and then they laughed at each other.

'Ours isn't a normal life, is it?' he shouted.

'Nope,' yelled back Gwen.

And they carried on climbing.

A long way below them and on a beach a few hundred miles to the left, the xXltttxtolxtol had gathered themselves in front of the portal, and were beginning a strange victory chant.

The portal began to spill out a rippling light and tendrils of Rift energy speared out, each one latching onto a xXltttxtolxtol, rooting it to the ground. The bridgehead was established.

Through the portal could be glimpsed shapes, rank after rank of sinister, spiky shadows.

Gwen glanced out of a porthole. All she could see outside was fire and clouds, which meant that they were getting closer and closer to the Earth. She really wondered how this was going to work out. And what it would feel like if it went wrong.

George turned to her, offering her a hand into the egg-shaped shuttlecraft. 'Come along, Gwen, dear,' he yelled. 'I think we're cutting it a little tight.'

Gwen leapt, hearing the door slam shut behind her. It was a snug fit on the inside of the egg, all button-upholstered velvet. George hurriedly pulled a lever, and the egg spun away from the doomed rocket ship.

As they tumbled over and over, Gwen noticed that gravity had pinned a fresh plate and a neat pile of cucumber sandwiches to the floor.

Up on the deck of the doomed ship, Bramwell's sensors noticed the departure of the shuttle with a sad regret, and then concentrated its dwindling resources on holding the rocket ship on a steady course to the planet below.

'I don't feel so good,' groaned Ianto. 'That rum…'

'You drank it?' laughed Agnes.

'Why?' murmured Ianto. 'What was I supposed to do?'

'Oh,' said Jack loudly. 'What with your head for spirits, I was just assuming you were pretending. We don't want a repeat of the Christmas party. The poor lamb threw up over a Weevil. Waste of a great single malt.'

'That was ninety per cent proof pure Bermudian,' laughed Agnes. 'I'm only sorry it's gone. Warms the heart magnificently.'

The dawn sky was spreading swiftly over the beach, an Athena poster spread of peaches and cherry reds.

'Shepherd's warning,' Agnes shook her head.

'I know,' sighed Jack. 'I always knew it would rain on the last day.'

Then they all noticed one star still in the sky, a star that was moving towards the beach very, very quickly.

'What?' murmured Ianto, blinking.

They heard a roaring noise and the blaring of a horn. And there, tearing across the beach towards them was a white van.

Jack looked up at the sky, and then at the van, and then at the xXltttxtolxtol. 'Gwen Cooper,' he said, quietly and appreciatively.

'Agreed,' nodded Agnes and stepped away from her bonds, followed by Jack.

Ianto stared at them. 'How?' he gasped.

Agnes rolled her eyes. 'Jack and I dissolved the tree sap with the alcohol whilst pretending to drink it. It also appears to have poisoned our captors. Harkness, free your Ganymede.'

The two of them reached over and started to prise Ianto away from his bonds.

The xXltttxtolxtol were just beginning to notice the approaching van when the air itself started to shake. They twisted around, trying to work out if it was the portal or not.

'Look up!' yelled Jack.

The xXltttxtolxtol looked up and saw the burning star hurtling towards the beach.

'No!' screamed zZxgbtl. 'The portal!' He and his troops twisted with indecision, but did not, could not move.

The van tore up to Agnes, Jack and Ianto. The side door was already open, and it didn't even stop. Rhys's face appeared at the window, yelling, 'Get in, get bloody in!'

The van roared away, with its passengers folded in an untidy heap of suit, greatcoat and hooped skirt. As it reached the edge of the beach and the wheels began to spin hopelessly on the pebbled gradient soaked with diesel, the Torchwood Institute's first ever rocket ship smashed down very neatly on top of Jack's phone.

The resulting explosion ignited the beach, the xXltttxtolxtol, their portal, and the highly flammable remains of the Vam.

'Howabout that then?' boomed Rhys, delightedly. 'That was some very nifty driving, even if I do say so myself.'

They were rattling across the deserted Penarth Road. In the distance, they could hear sirens.

'Rhys,' said Jack, sliding into the passenger seat next to him. 'Well done. Where are we going?'

'Oh ah,' said Rhys casually. 'Just promised I'd give the wife a lift home.'

They parked in the next-door bay, where a large metal egg lay on its side. Leaning against it were Gwen and a man in neatly old-fashioned clothes. They were sharing a plate of sandwiches.

Gwen waved as they drew up.

Agnes rushed from the van, pecked Gwen quickly on the cheek, and then hugged George Herbert Sanderson tightly. Gwen ran over to Rhys and grabbed him before he even made it out of the van.

'Aw,' Jack smiled and turned to Ianto, but found him

throwing up behind a sand dune. Jack went and patted him on the shoulder.

'Never let me drink rum again,' Ianto wailed.

'Don't worry, I won't.' Jack rubbed his hair, and then, cradling him in his arms, walked him back to the others. 'This,' he said to the beach in general, 'is a great spot for a picnic. Let's bunk off. It's going to be a lovely day.'

And then it started to rain.

XVIII

AN APPEARANCE
IN THE MARSHALSEA

In which Mrs Cooper receives a shock, and Miss Havisham has
the last word

*She was surprised to find herself pulled from the rubble by a
handsome stranger.*

*All around her, she could see debris poking up through the
earth. And occasionally, distressingly, a scrap of clothing.*

*'Well,' she said, 'it appears we have been lucky. We're the only
survivors.'*

*The man grinned and shook his head. 'Not lucky. I protected
you from the blast.'*

*She inclined her head. 'In that case, you have my gratitude. You
could have been killed.'*

*The man shrugged, and widened his grin. 'Who's to say I
wasn't, ma'am?'*

*She let herself smile slightly at the witticism. 'Such good
manners. And, I believe, you're an American?'*

He nodded. 'Only just joined.'

*She gestured at the ruined building. 'Not every day is like this, I
assure you. Wednesdays are reliably unremarkable.'*

'Noted,' he said.

'Forgive me,' she said, feeling a polite impulse. 'You've saved my life, but you haven't told me your name.'

He smirked, a little forwardly, she thought. 'Captain Jack Harkness,' he said. 'Hello!'

She stuck out a gloved hand. 'Then welcome to Torchwood, Captain Harkness. I'm sure we're going to get on famously.'

They were back at the Hub. Rhys had gone home to watch footage of the burning beach on the news. Agnes had insisted that George Herbert Sanderson go down to the cells, 'pending his debriefing'. She had ordered everyone else to the Boardroom.

She had even made tea.

As they walked in, she looked calmly at all of them. At Ianto, slightly green in the face, but somehow still neat in his crumpled suit, Jack buoyed and smug in his greatcoat, and Gwen battered, hair all out of place, and clothes burnt and torn.

'I'll be mother,' Agnes said, pouring and handing round cups.

There was a moment of silence as she watched them all, smiling broadly. The moment stretched a little, and Ianto coughed awkwardly.

'Well,' she said. 'My assessment is at an end.'

'Oh come on!' protested Jack. 'You can't seriously still be—'

'Captain Harkness,' continued Agnes, with a touch of her old steel, 'I have a function to perform. You might argue that it is all I have left. It is my job to assess how well Torchwood functions under your command. And to that end, I have observed all of your performances against the tests that I have devised.'

'What?' gasped Ianto.

Agnes smiled at him sweetly.

'Oh, so that's it,' laughed Jack bitterly. 'You nearly destroy the world twice, and then you claim that it was all a test? That's rich! Not even you can pull that one off – you, my lady, are going back to Swindon and I'm locking you up for good!'

Gwen hushed him, frantically mouthing 'Cowper Key' at him. One word and Agnes could seal them in the Hub. It was important that Jack didn't forget that now. 'Er… what Jack means to say,' she said gently, 'is that it's been a taxing few days.'

'Oh, of course,' Agnes beamed. 'Testing, you might say.'

'You're going to let her get away with it,' murmured Jack under his breath.

Gwen silenced him again. 'And that we're all naturally interested to know the outcome of your assessment. Both for us, and, of course, for George Herbert.'

'Ah, indeed,' smiled Agnes. 'Well, naturally he must be thoroughly debriefed. I am not immediately satisfied over his conduct in this affair. He will not escape scot-free. And, indeed, if there are questions arising over my own behaviour, then they, naturally, must also be held to account. But there are more immediate and pressing

233

matters.' She tapped a folder beneath her hand. 'This is my dossier on your assessment. And I have to say that, while a lot has alarmed and worried me, overall I must admit I am very impressed by your performance…'

Jack puffed himself up.

'… Mrs Cooper.'

'What?' Jack barked.

'Quite,' said Agnes, looking at Gwen with a smile. 'Torchwood has a long history of brilliant leadership under messy but imaginative women. And I truly believe that you are one such. Gwen Cooper, I am putting you in charge.'

'Um,' said Gwen, looking around the room. Jack was a shade of purple, Ianto was stirring his tea over and over again.

'No, no, my dear, don't thank me. Harkness has done wonderful work for Torchwood in his day, to be sure, but the time has come for a fresh grip on the reins, I'm sure you'll all agree.'

Jack stood up, glared at Agnes, and then sat down.

'I firmly believe that the moment has come for Jack to offer more of an executive, consultative role, perhaps even return to a freelance basis. Under you, Mrs Cooper, Gwen dear, I truly believe that the twenty-first century can be when everything changes for the better.'

Agnes stood, indicating the folder on the desk. 'It's all here in more detail, but it has been a true privilege working with you. I shall be in my office if you require any clarification.'

She swept from the room.

There was stunned silence for ten seconds.

Gwen sat on her hands.

'Congratulations,' muttered Jack, not looking at her.

'Oh, come on,' protested Gwen, blushing. 'It's… er… she's… Well, look, it's not like what she says is enforceable.' She stood up and crossed over to Jack, who spun his chair away from her. 'Honestly, Jack. This is all her way of setting us against each other. She just doesn't want us coming back at her for nearly getting the Earth invaded. Once she's gone, it'll be business as usual. Jack,' she said soothingly. 'You are Torchwood.'

Jack murmured something.

'Gwen has a point,' said Ianto reasonably and sadly. He opened the folder and then closed it again hurriedly.

'I think that's intended for me,' said Gwen quickly, and then apologised. 'I'm sorry, Ianto, I mean Jack, if you wouldn't mind me having a look?'

Jack made a theatrical gesture. 'Oh, be my guest, Gwen Cooper, sir.'

'Don't be like that,' said Gwen.

Ianto slid the folder across the desk.

Gwen paused.

She opened the folder.

'Oh,' she said.

'It's blank,' said Ianto.

Jack laughed.

'What does it mean?' asked Gwen, staring at the blank sheets of paper in the folder.

Jack drank his tea with a grimace before replying. 'I think you put your finger on it. It's about setting us against each other, boss.'

Gwen stood up. 'Stop that. And what do you mean?'

'You tell us.' Jack's tone was sweetly sour.

Gwen sipped her tea and grimaced. 'Eurch, no offence, Ianto, but this tea tastes worse than yours. It's vile.'

'I know,' said Ianto sadly. 'That'll be the Retcon.'

'What?' Jack spat out a mouthful. And that's when the alarms went off. He ran over to a monitor. 'Total systems shutdown! No! No! No! She's used the Key!' He bolted from the room.

'What do you mean, Retcon?' Gwen yelled at Ianto, before running after Jack.

Woozily, Ianto stood up, glanced again at the empty folder, giggled, and then walked unsteadily from the room.

They stood in the Hub, leaning against each other as the drug began to take effect. As the Torchwood systems shut down, the whole chamber was bathed in a pulsing red light.

They'd arrived just in time to see Agnes and George standing together high up on the invisible lift, gliding towards the tiny patch of sky that was Cardiff Bay. Agnes was smiling and waving.

'I am not amused,' said Jack.

And then the lights went out.

Acknowledgements

Miss Havisham respectfully presents her compliments to Mr Davies, Mr Tribe and Mr Russell, while gratefully acknowledging the assistance of Miss Raynor, Miss Seaborne, Mr Lidster and Mr Binding.

She also tenders her sincerest gratitude to Mr Minchin for the loan of the speedboat.

TORCHWOOD

Also available from BBC Books

TORCHWOOD
ANOTHER LIFE
Peter Anghelides

ISBN 978 0 563 48653 4
£6.99

Thick black clouds are blotting out the skies over Cardiff. As twenty-four inches of rain fall in twenty-four hours, the city centre's drainage system collapses. The capital's homeless are being murdered, their mutilated bodies left lying in the soaked streets around the Blaidd Drwg nuclear facility.

Tracked down by Torchwood, the killer calmly drops eight storeys to his death. But the killings don't stop. Their investigations lead Jack Harkness, Gwen Cooper and Toshiko Sato to a monster in a bathroom, a mystery at an army base and a hunt for stolen nuclear fuel rods. Meanwhile, Owen Harper goes missing from the Hub, when a game in *Second Reality* leads him to an old girlfriend...

Something is coming, forcing its way through the Rift, straight into Cardiff Bay.

Featuring Captain Jack Harkness as played by John Barrowman, with Gwen Cooper, Owen Harper, Toshiko Sato and Ianto Jones as played by Eve Myles, Burn Gorman, Naoki Mori and Gareth David-Lloyd, in the hit series created by Russell T Davies for BBC Television.

TORCHWOOD
BORDER PRINCES
Dan Abnett

ISBN 978 0 563 48654 1
£6.99

The End of the World began on a Thursday night in October, just after eight in the evening…

The Amok is driving people out of their minds, turning them into zombies and causing riots in the streets. A solitary diner leaves a Cardiff restaurant, his mission to protect the Principal leading him to a secret base beneath a water tower. Everyone has a headache, there's something in Davey Morgan's shed, and the church of St Mary-in-the-Dust, demolished in 1840, has reappeared – though it's not due until 2011. Torchwood seem to be out of their depth. What will all this mean for the romance between Torchwood's newest members?

Captain Jack Harkness has something more to worry about: an alarm, an early warning, given to mankind and held – inert – by Torchwood for 108 years. And now it's flashing. Something is coming. Or something is already here.

Featuring Captain Jack Harkness as played by John Barrowman, with Gwen Cooper, Owen Harper, Toshiko Sato and Ianto Jones as played by Eve Myles, Burn Gorman, Naoki Mori and Gareth David-Lloyd, in the hit series created by Russell T Davies for BBC Television.

Also available from BBC Books

T O R C H W O O D
SLOW DECAY
Andy Lane

ISBN 978 0 563 48655 8
£6.99

When Torchwood track an energy surge to a Cardiff nightclub, the team finds the police are already at the scene. Five teenagers have died in a fight, and lying among the bodies is an unfamiliar device. Next morning, they discover the corpse of a Weevil, its face and neck eaten away, seemingly by human teeth. And on the streets of Cardiff, an ordinary woman with an extraordinary hunger is attacking people and eating her victims.

The job of a lifetime it might be, but working for Torchwood is putting big strains on Gwen's relationship with Rhys. While she decides to spice up their love life with the help of alien technology, Rhys decides it's time to sort himself out – better music, healthier food, lose some weight. Luckily, a friend has mentioned Doctor Scotus's weight-loss clinic…

Featuring Captain Jack Harkness as played by John Barrowman, with Gwen Cooper, Owen Harper, Toshiko Sato and Ianto Jones as played by Eve Myles, Burn Gorman, Naoki Mori and Gareth David-Lloyd, in the hit series created by Russell T Davies for BBC Television.

Dr Bob Strong's GP surgery has been treating a lot of coughs and colds recently, far more than is normal for the time of year. Bob thinks there's something up but he can't think what. He seems to have caught it himself, whatever it is – he's starting to cough badly and there are flecks of blood in his hanky.

Saskia Harden has been found on a number of occasions submerged in ponds or canals but alive and seemingly none the worse for wear. Saskia is not on any files, except in the medical records at Dr Strong's GP practice.

But Torchwood's priorities lie elsewhere: investigating ghostly apparitions in South Wales, they have found a dead body. It's old and in an advanced state of decay. And it is still able to talk.

And what it is saying is 'Water hag'…

Featuring Captain Jack Harkness as played by John Barrowman, with Gwen Cooper, Owen Harper, Toshiko Sato and Ianto Jones as played by Eve Myles, Burn Gorman, Naoki Mori and Gareth David-Lloyd, in the hit series created by Russell T Davies for BBC Television.

Tiger Bay, Cardiff, 1953. A mysterious crate is brought into the docks on a Scandinavian cargo ship. Its destination: the Torchwood Institute. As the crate is offloaded by a group of local dockers, it explodes, killing all but one of them, a young Butetown lad called Michael Bellini.

Fifty-five years later, a radioactive source somewhere inside the Hub leads Torchwood to discover the same Michael Bellini, still young and dressed in his 1950s clothes, cowering in the vaults. They soon realise that each has encountered Michael before – as a child in Osaka, as a junior doctor, as a young police constable, as a new recruit to Torchwood One. But it's Jack who remembers him best of all.

Michael's involuntary time-travelling has something to do with a radiation-charged relic held inside the crate. And the Men in Bowler Hats are coming to get it back.

Featuring Captain Jack Harkness as played by John Barrowman, with Gwen Cooper, Owen Harper, Toshiko Sato and Ianto Jones as played by Eve Myles, Burn Gorman, Naoki Mori and Gareth David-Lloyd, in the hit series created by Russell T Davies for BBC Television.

Also available from BBC Books

T O R C H W O O D
THE TWILIGHT STREETS
Gary Russell

ISBN 978 1 846 07439 4
£6.99

There's a part of the city that no one much goes to, a collection of rundown old houses and gloomy streets. No one stays there long, and no one can explain why – something's not quite right there.

Now the Council is renovating the district, and a new company is overseeing the work. There will be street parties and events to show off the newly gentrified neighbourhood: clowns and face-painters for the kids, magicians for the adults – the street entertainers of Cardiff, out in force.

None of this is Torchwood's problem. Until Toshiko recognises the sponsor of the street parties: Bilis Manger.

Now there is something for Torchwood to investigate. But Captain Jack Harkness has never been able to get into the area; it makes him physically ill to go near it. Without Jack's help, Torchwood must face the darker side of urban Cardiff alone…

Featuring Captain Jack Harkness as played by John Barrowman, with Gwen Cooper, Owen Harper, Toshiko Sato and Ianto Jones as played by Eve Myles, Burn Gorman, Naoki Mori and Gareth David-Lloyd, in the hit series created by Russell T Davies for BBC Television.

Also available from BBC Books

TORCHWOOD
PACK ANIMALS
Peter Anghelides

ISBN 978 1 846 07574 2
£6.99

Shopping for wedding gifts is enjoyable, unless like Gwen you witness a Weevil massacre in the shopping centre. A trip to the zoo is a great day out, until a date goes tragically wrong and Ianto is badly injured by stolen alien tech. And Halloween is a day of fun and frights, before unspeakable monsters invade the streets of Cardiff and it's no longer a trick or a treat for the terrified population.

Torchwood can control small groups of scavengers, but now someone has given large numbers of predators a season ticket to Earth. Jack's investigation is hampered when he finds he's being investigated himself. Owen is convinced that it's just one guy who's toying with them. But will Torchwood find out before it's too late that the game is horribly real, and the deck is stacked against them?

Featuring Captain Jack Harkness as played by John Barrowman, with Gwen Cooper, Owen Harper, Toshiko Sato and Ianto Jones as played by Eve Myles, Burn Gorman, Naoki Mori and Gareth David-Lloyd, in the hit series created by Russell T Davies for BBC Television.

T O R C H W O O D
SKYPOINT
Phil Ford

ISBN 978 1 846 07575 9
£6.99

'If you're going to be anyone in Cardiff, you're going to be at SkyPoint!'

SkyPoint is the latest high-rise addition to the ever-developing Cardiff skyline. It's the most high-tech, avant-garde apartment block in the city. And it's where Rhys Williams is hoping to find a new home for himself and Gwen. Gwen's more concerned by the money behind the tower block – Besnik Lucca, a name she knows from her days in uniform.

When Torchwood discover that residents have been going missing from the tower block, one of the team gets her dream assignment. Soon SkyPoint's latest newly married tenants are moving in. And Toshiko Sato finally gets to make a home with Owen Harper.

Then something comes out of the wall…

Featuring Captain Jack Harkness as played by John Barrowman, with Gwen Cooper, Owen Harper, Toshiko Sato and Ianto Jones as played by Eve Myles, Burn Gorman, Naoki Mori and Gareth David-Lloyd, in the hit series created by Russell T Davies for BBC Television.

T O R C H W O O D
ALMOST PERFECT
James Goss

ISBN 978 1 846 07573 5
£6.99

Emma is 30, single and frankly desperate. She woke up this morning with nothing to look forward to but another evening of unsuccessful speed-dating. But now she has a new weapon in her quest for Mr Right. And it's made her almost perfect.

Gwen Cooper woke up this morning expecting the unexpected. As usual. She went to work and found a skeleton at a table for two and a colleague in a surprisingly glamorous dress. Perfect.

Ianto Jones woke up this morning with no memory of last night. He went to work, where he caused amusement, suspicion and a little bit of jealousy. Because Ianto Jones woke up this morning in the body of a woman. And he's looking just about perfect.

Jack Harkness has always had his doubts about Perfection.

Featuring Captain Jack Harkness as played by John Barrowman, with Gwen Cooper and Ianto Jones as played by Eve Myles and Gareth David-Lloyd, in the hit series created by Russell T Davies for BBC Television.

TORCHWOOD
INTO THE SILENCE
Sarah Pinborough

ISBN 978 1 846 07753 1
£6.99

The body in the church hall is very definitely dead. It has been sliced open with surgical precision, its organs exposed, and its vocal cords are gone. It is as if they were never there or they've been dissolved…

With the Welsh Amateur Operatic Contest getting under way, music is filling the churches and concert halls of Cardiff. The competition has attracted the finest Welsh talent to the city, but it has also drawn something else – there are stories of a metallic creature hiding in the shadows. Torchwood are on its tail, but it's moving too fast for them to track it down.

This new threat requires a new tactic – so Ianto Jones is joining a male voice choir…

Featuring Captain Jack Harkness as played by John Barrowman, with Gwen Cooper and Ianto Jones as played by Eve Myles and Gareth David-Lloyd, in the hit series created by Russell T Davies for BBC Television.

TORCHWOOD
BAY OF THE DEAD
Mark Morris

ISBN 978 1 846 07737 1
£6.99

When the city sleeps, the dead start to walk…

Something has sealed off Cardiff, and living corpses are stalking the streets, leaving a trail of half-eaten bodies. Animals are butchered. A young couple in their car never reach their home. A stolen yacht is brought back to shore, carrying only human remains. And a couple of girls heading back from the pub watch the mysterious drivers of a big black SUV take over a crime scene.

Torchwood have to deal with the intangible barrier surrounding Cardiff, and some unidentified space debris that seems to be regenerating itself. Plus, of course, the all-night zombie horror show.

Not that they really believe in zombies.

Featuring Captain Jack Harkness as played by John Barrowman, with Gwen Cooper and Ianto Jones as played by Eve Myles and Gareth David-Lloyd, in the hit series created by Russell T Davies for BBC Television.

T O R C H W O O D
THE HOUSE THAT JACK BUILT
Guy Adams

ISBN 978 1 846 07739 5
£6.99

Jackson Leaves – an Edwardian house in Penylan, built 1906, semi-detached, three storeys, spacious, beautifully presented. Left in good condition to Rob and Julia by Rob's late aunt.

It's an ordinary sort of a house. Except for the way the rooms don't stay in the same places. And the strange man that turns up in the airing cupboard. And the apparitions. And the temporal surges that attract the attentions of Torchwood.

And the fact that the first owner of Jackson Leaves in 1906 was a Captain Jack Harkness…

Featuring Captain Jack Harkness as played by John Barrowman, with Gwen Cooper and Ianto Jones as played by Eve Myles and Gareth David-Lloyd, in the hit series created by Russell T Davies for BBC Television.

TORCHWOOD
RISK ASSESSMENT
James Goss

ISBN 978 1 846 07783 8

£6.99

'Are you trying to tell me, Captain Harkness, that the entire staff of Torchwood Cardiff now consists of yourself, a woman in trousers and a tea boy?'

Agnes Haversham is awake, and Jack is worried (and not a little afraid). The Torchwood Assessor is roused from her deep sleep in only the worst of times – it's happened just four times in the last 100 years. Can the situation really be so bad?

Someone, somewhere, is fighting a war, and they're losing badly. The coffins of the dead are coming through the Rift. With thousands of alien bodies floating in the Bristol Channel, it's down to Torchwood to round them all up before a lethal plague breaks out.

And now they'll have to do it by the book. The 1901 edition.

Featuring Captain Jack Harkness as played by John Barrowman, with Gwen Cooper and Ianto Jones as played by Eve Myles and Gareth David-Lloyd, in the hit series created by Russell T Davies for BBC Television.

Also available from BBC Books

T O R C H W O O D
THE UNDERTAKER'S GIFT
Trevor Baxendale

ISBN 978 1 846 07782 1
£6.99

The Hokrala Corp lawyers are back. They're suing planet Earth for mishandling the twenty-first century, and they won't tolerate any efforts to repel them. An assassin has been sent to remove Captain Jack Harkness.

It's been a busy week in Cardiff. The Hub's latest guest is a translucent, amber jelly carrying a lethal electrical charge. Record numbers of aliens have been coming through the Rift, and Torchwood could do without any more problems.

But there are reports of an extraordinary funeral cortège in the night-time city, with mysterious pallbearers guarding a rotting cadaver that simply doesn't want to be buried.

Torchwood should be ready for anything – but with Jack the target of an invisible killer, Gwen trapped in a forgotten crypt and Ianto Jones falling desperately ill, could a world of suffering be the Undertaker's gift to planet Earth?

Featuring Captain Jack Harkness as played by John Barrowman, with Gwen Cooper and Ianto Jones as played by Eve Myles and Gareth David-Lloyd, in the hit series created by Russell T Davies for BBC Television.

TORCHWOOD
CONSEQUENCES
James Moran, Joseph Lidster, Andrew Cartmel, Sarah Pinborough and David Llewellyn

ISBN 978 1 846 07784 5
£6.99

Saving the planet, watching over the Rift, preparing the human race for the twenty-first century... Torchwood has been keeping Cardiff safe since the late 1800s. Small teams of heroes, working 24/7, encountering and containing the alien, the bizarre and the inexplicable.

But Torchwood do not always see the effects of their actions. What links the Rules and Regulations for replacing a Torchwood leader to the destruction of a shopping centre? How does a witness to an alien's reprisals against Torchwood become caught up in a night of terror in a university library? And why should Gwen and Ianto's actions at a local publishers have a cost for Torchwood more than half a century earlier?

For Torchwood, the past will always catch up with them. And sometimes the future will catch up with the past...

Featuring Captain Jack Harkness as played by John Barrowman, with Gwen Cooper and Ianto Jones as played by Eve Myles and Gareth David-Lloyd, and Owen Harper and Toshiko Sato as played by Burn Gorman and Naoki Mori in the hit series created by Russell T Davies for BBC Television.

THE
T O R C H W O O D
ARCHIVES

ISBN 978 1 846 07459 2
£14.99

Separate from the Government
Outside the police
Beyond the United Nations…

Founded by Queen Victoria in 1879, the Torchwood Institute has long battled against alien threats to the British Empire. *The Torchwood Archives* is an insider's look into the secret world of this unique investigative team.

In-depth background on personnel, case files on alien enemies of the Crown and descriptions of extra-terrestrial technology collected over the years will uncover more about the world of Torchwood than ever previously known, including some of the biggest mysteries surrounding the Rift in space and time running through Cardiff.

Based on the hit series created by Russell T Davies for BBC Television.

T O R C H W O O D
THE ENCYCLOPEDIA
Gary Russell

ISBN 978 1 846 07764 7
£14.99

Founded by Queen Victoria in 1879, the Torchwood Institute has been defending Great Britain from the alien hordes for 130 years. Though London's Torchwood One was destroyed during the Battle of Canary Wharf, the small team at Torchwood Three have continued to monitor the space-time Rift that runs through Cardiff, saving the world and battling for the future of the human race.

Now you can discover every fact and figure, explore every crack in time and encounter every creature that Torchwood have dealt with. Included here are details of:

- The secret of the Children of Earth

- Operatives from Alice Guppy to Gwen Cooper

- Extraterrestrial visitors from Arcateenians to Weevils

- The life and deaths of Captain Jack Harkness

and much more. Illustrated throughout with photos and artwork from all three series, this A–Z provides everything you need to know about Torchwood.

Based on the hit series created by Russell T Davies for BBC Television.